Love,
Football,
And Other
Contact
Sports

LOVE, FOOTBALL, AND OTHER CONTACT SPORTS

ALDEN R. CARTER

Holiday House / New York

ACKNOWLEDGMENTS

Many thanks to all who helped with *Love, Football, and Other Contact Sports,* particularly my son, Brian (CB), his teammates Cory Helwig (TE), Corey Geldernick (RB), Shawn Handke (WR), Ben King (QB), Ben "Cookie" Corcoran (OT), and Mike Ott (WR). Thanks also to defensive backfield coach Jerry Littman, head coach Len Luedtke, and WDLB football analyst Dale Yakaites. Although some of the 2001 Marshfield Tigers lent a quirk or some physical bulk to a characterization, none of these fine young people should be confused with any character in the book.

Thanks also to my daughter, Siri; my wife, Carol; my agent, Bill Reiss; and my editor, Regina Griffin.

This project was supported in part by a grant from the Wisconsin Arts Board with funds from the state of Wisconsin.

Several stories in *Love, Football, and Other Contact Sports* originally appeared in whole or in part in the following publications and are published herein with permission or in accordance with rights retained by Alden R. Carter under the terms of the original contracts: "A Good Game" and "The Gully" in *Scholastic Scope* (Oct. 5, 1998, and March 21, 1997); "Pig Brains" in *On the Edge: Stories at the Brink,* edited by Lois Duncan (Simon & Schuster, 1999); "Satyagraha" in *On the Fringe,* edited by Donald R. Gallo (Dial, 2001); and "Trashback" in *No Easy Answers: Short Stories about Teenagers Making Tough Choices,* edited by Donald R. Gallo (Bantam Doubleday Dell, 1997).

Library of Congress Cataloging-in-Publication Data

Carter, Alden R.
    Love, football, and other contact sports / by Alden R. Carter.—1st ed.
    p. cm.
    Summary: A collection of stories about high school students from one end of the social spectrum to the other.
    Contents: Love, football, and other contact sports—Trashback—Pig brains—Buck's head—Satyagraha—Elvis—The ogre of Mensa—The gully—Kicker wanted—The briefcase—Jersey day—Big Chicago——The ghost of Mum-mum—The Doughnut boots his reputation—A good game.
    ISBN-13: 978-0-8234-1975-3
    ISBN-10: 0-8234-1975-4
    1. Children's stories, American. [1. High schools—Fiction. 2. Schools—Fiction.
3. Short stories.] I. Title.
PZ7.C2426Lov 2005
[Fic]—dc22   2005046094

For my son, Brian, and
his coaches and teammates
of the 2001 Marshfield Tigers,
winners of the Division 1
Wisconsin State Football Championship

CONTENTS

STORIES FROM SENIOR YEAR

A GIRL'S GUIDE TO FOOTBALL PLAYERS

by the female
editorial staff of the
*Purple Cow Literary
Magazine*

*Milking Creativity
in Psychedelic Color*

oFFENSIVE TEAM

Offensive Linemen (subspecies: center, 1; guards, 2; tackles, 2). Large people who get in the way of (*block*) the large people on the defensive team. The **center** chucks the ball through his legs (a *hike* or *snap*) to the quarterback. The center and the rest of the linemen then attempt to keep the quarterback and running backs from being killed. In this effort, they cannot grab a defensive player. This is called *holding*, a penalty that invariably results in fervent denials by linemen, great wailing and weeping among fans, and much profanity from coaches. Very smelly and dirty by the end of the game. Clean up fairly well and keep fairly orderly cars (or pickup trucks). Tend to hang together off the field, yelling stupid mottos like "Band of Brothers" or "All for One and One for All."

Quarterback: Numero uno—as he'll remind you—player on offense. Small enough to hide behind offensive linemen. Starts play by goosing center from behind. Yells a lot of gibberish prior to receiving the ball from the center, whereupon he tries to get rid of it as quickly as possible by handing it to a running back (a *handoff*) or heaving it to a receiver (a *pass*). Occasionally fails to accomplish either and is brutalized by defensive players (a *sack*). Can enliven a dull game by dropping the ball (a *fumble*) or throwing it to a defensive player (an *interception*). After a victory, talks exclusively about himself. After a loss, whines continuously about the failings of other players. Is never himself at fault. Good points:

cleans up on his own, spends money on dates, and drives a sporty car that his mother runs through the car wash twice a week.

Receivers (subspecies: wide receivers, 2; tight end, 1). Catch the ball. **Wide receivers** tend to be tall, stringy, fast guys. Must be egotistical enough to consider themselves invulnerable to injury. Off the field tend to brood about missed catches. Expect to hear frequent repetitions of "If only . . ." Otherwise, pretty presentable. Usually drive the family car, but it's a nice one.

A distinct subspecies is the **tight end**, who is larger and usually somewhat dimmer than wide receivers. He sometimes blocks like an offensive lineman, and sometimes catches (or drops) passes like a wide receiver. In a more advanced organism, this role confusion might lead to an identity crisis or even schizophrenia, but the tight end makes do with a state of perpetual perplexity. Tends to clean up less well than other offensive players. For reasons yet undetermined, clings fiercely to an ancient pickup truck with a stupid nickname like Road Warrior or the Green Hammer.

Running backs (subspecies: tailback [smallish], 1; fullback [larger], 1). Carry the ball or block. The **tailback** does more of the former, the **fullback** more of the latter. The smallest players to actually move toward the line of play where large people are trying to hurt one another. Ideally, the running back with the ball dodges through the mess and runs as fast as he can down the field. Off the field, the tailback cleans up well, the fullback less well. Their cars are a few years old but generally respectable.

OFFENSIVE TEAM

Defensive linemen (subspecies: tackles, 2; defensive ends, 2). Usually a little smaller than offensive linemen but meaner. Generally a walking bad attitude. Try to hurt anyone in their way, especially the person with the ball. (If a defensive player tackles the player with the ball in the end zone, this is called a *safety* and is worth two points. The offensive team must then kick to the opposing team.) Clean up poorly. Own messy four-wheel-drive pickup trucks. Usually hunt or work on stock cars in spare time. Best handled by country girls who know how to gut dead animals.

Linebackers (subspecies: none, thank God). Smaller but even meaner than defensive linemen. Line up behind the defensive line to rush the quarterback or tackle the running back. Consider spilled blood and broken bones (including their own) great sources of amusement. Nearly impossible to make presentable without sedation or electroshock therapy. Drive aging muscle cars littered with fast-food wrappers. Pathologies aside, may occasionally demonstrate faint signs of intelligence.

Defensive backs (subspecies: cornerbacks, 2; free safety, 1; strong safety, 1). Try to keep receivers from catching the ball. Except for the kicker, usually smallest guys on the field. Often seen running away from where large people are beating on each other. Hence, may be considered among the most intelligent players on the field. The exception is the **strong safety**, who really would rather be a linebacker. **Cornerbacks** and the **free safety** clean up well, often without direction. The strong safety requires more work. Cornerbacks and the free safety drive compact or subcompact cars that they like to think of as sporty but that they actually bought for the good gas mileage. When his driver's license isn't suspended, the strong safety rides a motorcycle.

sPECIAL TEAMs

Kicker. Can be identified by his clean uniform, small size, nervous tics, and a perplexed frown that seems to be asking, "What am I doing here?" Kicks the ball as far as he can (a *kickoff*) to start the game. He will then jog down the field, hoping to avoid any further involvement in the play, an exceedingly intelligent thing to do leading the casual observer to wonder what mental aberration caused him to engage in a contact sport with large people in the first place. Kicks (or misses) an *extra point* following a touchdown. Will occasionally attempt a three-point kick (a *field goal*) when the offense cannot otherwise get the ball into the end zone. Wildly ecstatic if he succeeds. Adopts an attitude of abject misery after missing a field goal or extra point in hopes of avoiding injury by large, angry teammates, who will nevertheless chastise him with blows to the helmet, shoulders, and backside. Off the field tends to be low-maintenance and self-cleaning. Drives his mother's minivan.

Holder. Holds the ball for the kicker on field goals and extra points. Often a job given to the backup quarterback to accustom him to game conditions and the sensation of having fingers dislocated.

Kick returner. A fast guy, usually a wide receiver, who catches the kickoff and runs it back up the field. This requires a suspension of all survival instincts, since the people coming the other way are all intent on killing him. Not a job for sissies or anyone with a lick of common sense.

Punter. Kicks the ball off the toe of his shoe to the other team when the offense fails to obtain a *first down* in three plays. (Note: plays are called *downs* and can be earned in groups of four by moving the ball ten yards or until the offensive team gets the ball over the *goal line* into the *end zone*. This scores a *touchdown*, worth six points.) The punter will occasionally get knocked down, whereupon he will roll around in real or simulated agony. If approached too closely by a defensive player, he will fall over and commence having convulsions in hopes of getting a penalty called for "roughing the kicker." Since he often plays another position during the rest of the game, off-field behavior is difficult to predict. However, people who offer an extended leg—no matter how briefly—for other people to tear off shouldn't be expected to demonstrate high cerebral functioning.

Punt returner. The kick returner can at least see death coming his way. But the punt returner must stand with his head thrown back, waiting for the punt to come down, while a herd of crazed Neanderthals comes thundering at him. Anecdotal evidence indicates that most punt returners quickly become extremely religious, using these brief moments in the traditional Returner's Prayer: *God, please don't let them kill me.* If the punt is short, he will wave his arm frantically in the air to signal a *fair catch*, a promise that if allowed to live he will only catch the ball and not try to go anyplace with it.

Long snapper. Hikes the ball to the punter on punts or to the holder on field goals and extra points. This task requires him to get his head as far as possible between his legs in order to aim. A millisecond later he is usually knocked butt over teakettle by a charging linebacker. This is a source of great hilarity for linebackers, who will then shout such witticisms as: "Hey, _____! Get your head out of your a__!"

A FOOTBALL PLAYER'S GUIDE TO LOVE

by the Argyle West
Football Team

Love. Well, you see it's, uh, sort of, you know, kinda like when . . . Hey, can we talk about this later?

KICKoff

(Or Never Trust a Girl
Who Steals Your
Ice-Cream Sandwich)

Sarah plucked the ice-cream sandwich from my fingers. "Hey!" I yelped. "Give me a break."

"Nope. The coaches want you to lose five pounds. I'm just helping out." She bit into the sandwich. "Hey, this is good."

"Sarah," I whined. "It's Hell Week. I need my energy." I tried to reach for the sandwich, but she stiff-armed me with her left hand.

"Careful, big guy. You wouldn't want me to get physical." She took another big bite.

"Just let me have half."

"Nope. Not even a bite." She bit into the sandwich again.

I slumped. "They ought to put you kids on the literary magazine through a Hell Week. Lock you in the gym for a week and make you write poetry or something."

"Hey, that sounds kind of fun. We could start with limericks." She recited:

"There was a young man named Kenneth
Who had a belly quite memmeth"

"Memmeth?" I said. "That's weak."

"Hush," she said. "This is just a rough draft." She frowned, the last bite of sandwich disappearing into her mouth.

"He ate ice cream all day
Five gallons I'd say
Now on the bench each game he remaineth."

"That is probably the worst poem ever written."

"Ha," she said, "you ought to see some of the stuff we get in. It's actually quite good compared to that junk. You know, that really tasted good. I think I'll get another one."

"Do, and you're walking home."

She leaned over and kissed me, her lips still sticky with ice cream. "Oh, you wouldn't do that."

"Try me," I said. I turned the ignition key, pumping the gas to get the Green Hammer revving. The Hammer is my aging Ford pickup, and I like it, dents, rust holes, and all. It has character.

Sarah looked out the rear window. "Blue smoke, captain. Air quality just dipped a point."

"It's not that bad." I dropped the truck into gear.

"So, how was day three of Hell Week?"

"Hell. I don't understand why seniors have to go through it. We've already proved we can play."

"Who's hot, who's not?"

"The Catman looks good. Wants everyone to know it, too. Rollin's doing okay. The Doughnut is bigger than ever. Matt Sommermeyer is kicking the absolute crap out of the ball. The defense . . . Well, they're hurting a little bit without Billy Patch. It's not easy to replace a three-time all-conference defensive end with ordinary mortals."

"I'm glad Matt's doing okay. I heard he tore up an ankle this summer."

"Yeah, he tipped over his four-wheeler. But that was his plant foot, and it seems fine now."

"So you offensive guys must feel good about the scrimmage tomorrow." She pronounced the word *offensive* like none of us used deodorant—actually more a characteristic of defensive players.

"Ha ha," I said. "You never get tired of that joke, do you?"

"It's definitely a keeper. You know, maybe I ought to do a whole series of limericks on the team. I bet that would boost sales of the magazine."

"Don't," I said, "I darned near got beaten to death last year when I stood up to Billy Patch. I don't want to take on the *whole* defense."

"I heard that you've got one new stud on defense. They call him 'Big' something."

"Big Chicago. Yeah, he's an animal all right. He's the new middle linebacker. Rollin's going to have his hands full getting him blocked tomorrow."

"How about you?"

"Oh, I won't see much of him. Tight ends don't run up against middle linebackers that much. But fullbacks see 'em plenty."

"How about when you're punting?"

"Chicago isn't on punt coverage, thank God. I wouldn't want that monster in my face while I'm trying to get off a kick. I don't know why the coaches gave me the job anyway."

"Is Rollin still the whatdoyacallit?"

"The long snapper. Yep, and Chicago would line up right over him on a rush." I turned onto her street.

Day four of Hell Week and the first day in pads. Suddenly everyone felt better. The uniform and equipment felt good after all the months since last season. Rollin Acres, my best buddy and possessor of the school's weirdest name, caught up to me as we jogged to the field. "I heard the coaches talking. They're going to put Chicago in on punt coverage."

"Ouch," I said. "Well, get a good block on him."

"With my head down between my legs?"

"Block him anyway."

"Easy for you to say. Get the ball off fast, that's my advice."

We ran through some drills and then huddled with Coach Carlson and the offensive coaches to start the scrimmage. "Okay, guys," Carlson said, "I'm expecting you to handle the defense, no sweat. Bill Patchet's gone. They don't have much experience in the line. The d-backs are rusty. So let's show them our stuff."

Someone in the back called, "How about Big Chicago, Coach?"

"He's just another ballplayer. Stick with the techniques you've learned, and you'll be fine."

"Coach," I said, "where'd this Big Chicago kid come from?"

"Chicago, I assume. He's a transfer student, that's all I know."

"How about the rumor he was all-conference as a junior?"

"I don't know. He's pretty good, but he's only one guy. Handle him."

Easier said than done. It wasn't that the guy was Superman, but he had a motor that didn't quit. He gave

Rollin a good lick on a fullback draw and twice broke through the line to hurry Marvin Katt, the Catman, into bad throws. Coach Carlson started getting on him. "For God's sake, Katt. Get rid of the ball. You can't stand there all day like we're playing the garden club."

Catman, who's got a *memmeth*-sized ego to go along with a major attitude problem, immediately started blaming his blockers and receivers. Two plays later, we had to punt.

As a junior, I'd been a distant third on the depth chart at punter. Then Jim Colburn graduated, and the coaches decided they wanted Matt Sommermeyer to stick to placekicking—which made me number one.

I was actually hoping some underclassman would beat me out. But nobody showed up who had any leg at all. "Well, Bauer," Coach Carlson said, "looks like you're our new punter."

"I don't know, Coach," I said, "Matt can kick it a lot farther than I can."

"Maybe. But we don't want to risk our placekicker on punting."

Oh, so it's okay to risk your starting tight end, I thought.

He slapped me on the shoulder. "You'll do fine. Confidence, lad, confidence."

But it was a tad difficult to be confident watching Big Chicago lining up to rush the punt. "Is there any truth to the story he hides a tire iron in his pants?" I asked Rollin when we broke the huddle.

"I'm guessing brass knuckles. He sure hit me with

something hard on that last draw play. God, I wish the coaches would stop calling that." He jogged forward to take his position over the ball.

I measured my steps back and checked my footing. Pat Sampson, the blocking back on the play, glanced back at me. "Ready, Ken?"

"Ready."

"Down!" Pat shouted. "Ready! Set! Hut . . . Hut . . ."

Chicago had it timed perfectly, hitting Rollin just as the ball sailed out between his legs. Rollin went tumbling. I had the ball, spun the laces, and tried to get it away as Chicago went airborne over Pat's low block. The ball came off my toe, thumping into Chicago's chest, and I went spinning as his outstretched arms slammed into my leg. We both scrambled for the ball. He scooped it up, but I got him around the thighs and put him down hard. Then we were up yelling at each other and pushing. "You psycho!" I shouted. "This is a scrimmage. That hit could have put me out for the year."

"I don't play scrimmages! I play football. You come to play against me and you'd better be ready to go to war." He shoved me hard. But I'm big and I don't go over easy. I hit right back just as hard.

Some of the players and coaches pulled us apart. Coach Carlson grabbed Chicago by the shoulder of his jersey and led him away. Chicago wrenched free and stood with his head bowed while Carlson yelled at him about the team, injuries, and using his damned head.

In the locker room, Coach Carlson shouted, "Bauer, over here." I went. He pointed at Chicago. "Now you two shake hands. Same school, same team. We hold our tempers and play clean. Now shake!"

I held out my hand. Chicago took it without enthusiasm or eye contact, then turned to his locker to get dressed. Carlson glared at his back, then patted me on the shoulder.

Sarah was waiting in the Hammer. "Did you see?" I asked.

"Oh, yeah. I thought I told you not to let him hurt you."

"He didn't. He could have, but I was lucky. God, I wonder what that kid's story is. He's a maniac."

"Maybe you ought to ask him."

"I'm not going to ask him crap."

"It might make a pretty good story."

"What do I care?"

"You like stories. That story you wrote about you, Rolf, and Fritz the Perverted Elf is pretty good."

"How do you know? I told you I was just messing around with it."

"I read it."

I looked at her hard. "Did you go digging into my backpack?"

"Well, the first part of practice was pretty boring, and I was hungry, so I looked in your backpack to see if you had a Snickers or something."

"You ate my Snickers?"

"Yep. You're on a diet, remember? And I read your story, since it happened to be sitting there begging for editorial comment."

I guess I could have gotten mad then, but first I had to ask, "And you thought it was pretty good, huh?"

"Well, not bad. It could use some work. A nip here, a tuck there, and you really ought to use a dictionary more."

"At least I don't use the word *memmeth* just to make a limerick work."

"Don't get defensive on me, big guy. Let me help you get it in shape, and we'll publish it in the next issue of the *Purple Cow.*"

"No way! I don't want people remembering all that junk about Fritz the Perverted Elf. I darn near got expelled for that."

"Oh, come on. That was two years ago. Nobody's going to worry about some stupid stuff you did as a sophomore. Besides, I think it's just the kind of story we need to sell more magazines. At least some of your jock friends will buy it."

I started to say something, but Sarah was on a roll.

"And if that story works, we'll start publishing a sports story in every issue."

"I don't have that many stories."

"You won't have to write them all. Other kids will submit stories. You can edit them."

"I thought you just said I couldn't spell."

"I'll lend you a dictionary." She reached over to muss my hair. "It'll be fun, Kenny."

I hesitated. "You really didn't think it was that bad, huh?"

"Not bad at all. A little overweight, a little rough around the edges—kinda like the guy who wrote it." She snuggled up. "And thoroughly lovable, just like you, big guy."

And what could I say to that?

STORIES FROM
SOPHOMORE YEAR

TRASHBACK

Featuring:

Ken Bauer, *tight end and class clown*

Rollin Acres, *fullback and straight man*

Rolf Egglehart, *vengeful nerd*

Sarah Landwehr, *sensible person*

Fritz the Perverted Elf, *height-challenged sexual deviant*

"... And the other nerd says, 'Hey, if you can guess how many chickens I've got in this bag, you can have *both* of 'em.'" I waited for the laughter. There wasn't much.

Mrs. Carruthers gave a tired sigh. "Exactly why, Kenneth, have you interrupted class with yet another of your tasteless nerd jokes?"

"Well, it's a grammar joke, Mrs. C. Kind of appropriate for English class, I thought."

"You thought wrong. Sarah, would you pick from the jar this time?"

Sarah shrugged and got up to select a slip of paper from the tall jar on the window ledge. I started to protest but swallowed it, as my beloved classmates—who I'd worked so hard to entertain—started hooting and laughing. Up at the front, Rolf Egglehart, the nerd's nerd, turned to give me what I suppose he thought was a sneer. It made him look more than ever like he needed to wipe his nose. I smiled evilly at him and made a gesture like I was wringing the neck of a chicken. He flushed and turned away.

Sarah took the top slip in the jar and read: "You're the elf in charge of answering Santa's mail. Write a letter that will get you fired, drive Santa to drink, and cause a police investigation of Santa's workshop."

"I can't do that one!" I yelped. "I mean, that's one I made up."

Almost everyone laughed. Sarah rolled her blue eyes to gaze up at the ceiling. Mrs. Carruthers, who I could tell wanted to give a hoot or two of her own, said, "Settle down, class. It is ironic, Kenneth, that Sarah happened to select your suggestion. But hoist upon your own petard or not, that is your assignment. Five hundred words should do it. By Monday, please."

Sarah looked at me and shook her head. I could interpret: Don't even ask me; I will not bail you out of this one.

As always, I rendezvoused at the cafeteria doors with Rollin. Three or four freshmen gave way to our size and genuine Argyle West football jerseys. "Heard you got in trouble with that chicken joke," Rollin said, slopping a second ladle of gravy on his mashed potatoes. "I thought that was a pretty good joke."

"You were supposed to like it," I said. "You're my straight man."

"I'm sick of being your straight man. Maybe I ought to tell the jokes for a while."

I shook my head. "Never work. Trust me on this one, Rollin. Anybody with parents dumb enough to name him Rollin Acres is a natural straight man."

He nodded sadly. "I suppose you're right. Do you think there's some kid out there whose parents were dumb enough to name him Rollin Stone?"

"Not a chance," I said.

"Too bad. That'd be kinda cool. So, what'd you get from the ol' penalty jar?"

"I got nailed. Remember when Sarah told us about the drama club's skit for the kiddies in the grade schools?"

"Oh, yeah. *Santa's Workshop.* And you wrote a slip about Santa's chief elf getting—"

"Right. That's the one I got. Serves me right."

He grimaced. "Ain't an easy one. What're you going to do?"

"Get Sarah to help me. What else?"

"One of these days, she's going to tell you to buzz off."

"Nah. I've known her since kindergarten. She always comes through. There she is. Come on."

Sarah looked up from the open book beside her tray. "Don't even start, Kenny! I do not want to hear about it. No whining, no pitiful looks. Write your own essay this time."

I sat down across from her and grinned. "Not to worry. Rollin and me got it all figured out. Just a matter of writing it up. We're going to do it next period in the computer lab."

"Well, keep the talk down. I'm the student supervisor next period."

"Sure. But, hey, Sarah. If you've got any suggestions, we'd be happy to listen."

She glared at me. "No! You're on your own."

I shrugged. "Sure. Not a problem." I dug into my lunch.

"Hmmmph," she said, and went back to reading her book.

Rollin got involved in a conversation with some kids at the other end of the table. "So," I said, "want to go out Saturday? Go to a movie or something?"

Sarah put her finger on her place in the book, gave a

tired sigh that Mrs. Carruthers would have envied, and stared at me. "Kenny, if you ever bothered to act your age, I might just say yes. But you don't, so it's still no, thanks."

"Hey," I said, "I'll start right now."

"Right. Think about your essay. I gotta go study."

Rollin and I gazed at the blank computer screen. "Well," Rollin said, "let 'er rip."

"I'm a stand-up," I said. "Funny stuff doesn't come to me sitting down."

"Stand up then."

"Can't write standing up."

"Then we've got a problem."

"Uh-huh," I said. I felt the back of my neck crawl and turned to catch Rolf watching us. I glared and he ducked back behind his computer. I let the front legs of my chair drop to the floor. "Well, here goes," I said. I typed:

Dear Mary,

I am Fritz, one of Santa's elves. Santa asked me to write to you. I am sorry, but we are not delivering any presents this year because the workshop elves are on strike.

"Boring," Rollin said. "Besides, why's he gonna get fired for writing that?"

"You're right," I said.

We stared at the screen for another couple of minutes. I began again:

Dear Mary,
 I'm Fritz, Santa's selfish elf. I'm supposed to tell
you that all your presents are coming. But none of
them are. Because I'm keeping them all. Ha, ha, ha.

"Still boring," Rollin said. "Maybe even worse."

I sighed, leaned back, and thought. "Okay, he's got to get fired."

"Right."

"Which means he's got to do something wrong."

"You're on the right track, Einstein."

"It's got to be something so bad that Santa starts drinking."

"Uh-huh."

"And the police come to investigate."

"Tall order," Rollin said.

"Yeah," I said, and started typing a third time:

Hey, Mary,
 I'm Fritz, Santa's perverted elf. I collect little girls'
panties. What color are yours? Maybe Christmas Eve,
when I ride with Santa, I'll ask if . . .

Rollin was laughing, and my fingers were moving about as fast as my so-so keyboard skills would take them. I kept on like that for a page or so. Nothing real, real bad. Just a lot of dumb stuff, but it was funny.

"Okay, what are you two clowns up to?" Sarah leaned over my shoulder to read the screen. After a few seconds, she slapped me on the back of the head.

"Ouch," I said, still giggling.

"Kenny, you are such a jerk, sometimes. And you, too, Rollin. You shouldn't encourage him."

"Oh, come on," I said. "We're just having a little fun. I'm not stupid enough to hand it in."

"You shouldn't even write it. You shouldn't even *think* it. Now erase that junk. Everything."

"I want a printout," Rollin said.

"Not on your life," she said. "Kenny, you dump that stuff right now."

"Okay, okay," I said. I dragged the file to the trash and punched the "empty" command. "It's gone."

Sarah fumed, glanced at the clock, sighed, and sat down at the computer beside me. "Rollin, go find something to do. I gotta straighten this kid out." She opened a new document. "Okay, quick outline." Her long fingers started moving on the keys. "Santa's broken some kind of environmental rule. Let's see." She brushed her blonde hair back from her cheek and chewed her lip for a moment. "Okay, he's using lead paint on the Christmas toys. Our elf hero blows the whistle. That may get him fired, but he thinks Santa isn't really responsible these days. Nipping the schnapps too much. So, our elf hero is willing to risk his job to protect the kiddies and get Santa some professional help. . . ."

She finished the outline, and it was a pretty good story. "Okay, you write it out, and we'll go over it tomorrow."

"Okay," I said, "but maybe it'd be simpler if you just—"

"No! I am not going to waste my evening doing your work."

"Just a suggestion," I said, but I was talking to her back. But it was a nice back.

That evening I used the PC at home to write the letter from Fritz, the whistle-blowing nerd elf, to Mary, brave daughter of the chief of Canada's environmental protection agency (a little detail I added). It was pretty funny, if I do say so myself. Not as funny as Fritz the perverted elf, but funny.

Sarah looked over my efforts the next afternoon. I sat close so I could smell her perfume until she slid her chair away a foot. "How can you spell so many words wrong when you've got a spell-checker?"

"Oops," I said. "Guess I forgot to run it."

She shook her head. "Did you bring the disk?"

"Sure thing." I grinned, knowing that she'd clean up more than just the spelling once she got started.

"You know," she said, as we waited for my disk to boot, "now that football's over, you might actually try to do something useful with all that comic energy."

"Like what?"

"Like join the drama club. We could use you in that Santa's workshop skit we're doing."

"Hey, I'm a stand-up. I don't want to be an elf."

She shook her head. "Kenny, you are not funny. You never were funny. All you do is get into trouble trying to be funny. And that makes me sad."

I was taken aback. Not because she didn't think I was funny. I mean, hey, there's no accounting for taste. But that she felt sad when I got in trouble? I mean, maybe a little embarrassed, sure, but *sad?* "Okay," I said. "I'll be an elf."

"And will you stop with the jokes, particularly in English class?"

I grimaced. "Well, I'll try. But did you hear about the nerd who—"

"No, and I don't want to!"

Anyway, that's how I became an elf. I tried to talk Rollin into becoming one, too. "Nothing much to it," I told him. "We go into a grade school, grab a few kids out of the audience to play parts, and then put on the skit."

"No way," he said. "Remember, I've got three little brothers. I *know* what little kids are like. And believe me, football's as rough a game as I want to play."

"Suit yourself. But I kinda like little kids; they're an easy audience. Besides, we get out of a lot of classes in the two or three weeks before Christmas."

"Come to think of it," Rollin said, "maybe it would be kind of fun to be an elf."

The next evening we were issued elf costumes—which were just a little tight in the crotch and shoulders, thank you—and started learning our parts.

Besides having the female lead, Sarah was Mr. Mc-Dunn's associate producer, which meant she'd be in charge any time we went to one of the grade schools while he was teaching. McDunn pointed to me. "Which elf are you, Bauer?"

"Fritz," I said, without thinking. Sarah gave me a warning look.

"There is no Fritz in the script. There's a Franz."

"That's what I meant."

We had our first performance two weeks later. It went pretty well, and we got better after that. Sarah (Mrs. Claus) and Bill Kappus (Santa) would select four kids from the audience and turn them over to Rollin and me. We'd rush them into the hall and jam them into costumes while Santa, Mrs. Claus, and the reindeer (two sophomores and two seminerd freshmen) sang a couple of Christmas songs with the remaining kids.

Because little kids come in a remarkable number of different sizes and shapes, getting them into their costumes took a lot of stuffing, tucking, and buckling. But the kids went along with it fine, liking my jokes and giggling when I tickled them. Then, *bam,* back on stage. Let the play begin.

I was having fun and doing a pretty darn good job. And not only with the play. My grades were up, and I hadn't gotten into trouble with a nerd joke in weeks. That's why I didn't expect anything bad when I was called to the principal's office ten minutes before afternoon homeroom the week before Christmas break.

"Hey, Mrs. G.," I said to the secretary. "What's up?"

She gave me a peculiar look. "Mr. Wenzel wants to see you in his office."

"Why?"

"You'll have to ask him. This way, please."

Not only Mr. Wenzel, but Mr. Mathias, the assistant principal, and Mr. McDunn, the drama coach, were waiting for me. Mr. Wenzel straightened in his chair. "Hello, Ken. Sit down, please."

"Uh, sure. What's going on?"

He studied me for a long moment. "We've received a copy of a rather disturbing letter. It's been alleged that you wrote it."

Alleged. What the heck was going on here? "Well, maybe," I said, "but I don't remember writing any letters recently. And certainly nothing disturbing. Unless, you mean, because I don't spell so good—"

He pushed a sheet of paper across his desk to me. "Did you write this?"

I read:

Hey, Mary,
    I'm Fritz, Santa's perverted elf. I collect little girls' panties. What color are . . .

"Hey," I blurted. "Where'd you get this?"

"Did you write it?"

"Yes . . . I mean, not exactly. Kind of. But, I never . . ." I took a deep breath. "Yes, I wrote it. But it was just me and a friend messing around in the computer lab before we got down to work. I didn't send it to anybody."

Mr. Mathias spoke. "Who is this Mary you were writing to?"

"No one! It was just a name we picked out. I picked out. Look, let me explain. . . ." I told them about telling the nerd joke in Mrs. Carruthers's class and then getting the extra writing assignment for wasting the class's time.

"So," Mr. Wenzel said, "you fancy yourself quite the class comedian."

"Well, a little, I guess. But not so much anymore. I've really enjoyed being in the drama club recently. It's been a lot of fun performing out there in the grade schools, and—"

"And it's just that involvement with youngsters that concerns us," Mr. Wenzel said. "Mr. McDunn tells us you are in physical contact with children before every performance."

I stared at him. "Hey, wait a second! I never touched one of those kids. I mean, yeah, I touched. I have to get them into their costumes. But I never touched one of them, you know, the wrong way. Who says I did?"

"No one. Or at least not yet. But it does concern us that you wrote—"

"Mr. Wenzel, that letter is dumb stuff. I was just trying to be funny. It doesn't have anything to do with how I feel about kids."

No one said anything for a minute. "So, who saw the letter?" Mr. Wenzel asked.

"Just me, my friend, and I guess one other friend. She told us we were jerks and that I ought to erase it. And I did. I don't know how anybody found it again, but it was gone when I finished at the computer."

"Who was the friend who helped you write it?"

I hesitated. "I'd rather not say."

"Why not?"

"I don't want to get him in trouble. He didn't really help write it. He just read it and laughed."

"Who was the girl who told you to erase it?"

I suddenly felt very cold. These guys were really trying to get me. Me and my friends. I leaned back. "I guess I'm not going to tell you that, either."

"Very well." He looked past me. "Mr. McDunn, I think you should plan on doing the rest of your performances without young Mr. Bauer's participation. Mr. Mathias, please get in contact with the grade schools. Don't upset anyone, but find out if there have been any reports of inappropriate behavior." He stared at me. "And, son, I don't think I'd have any contact with children until we get this cleared up."

I leaned against my locker, too dazed to move amid the tumult of kids shouting, laughing, and generally enjoying the heck out of Friday afternoon. How had this happened? I'd trashed that letter. Closed the document, dragged the icon to the trash, and then dumped the trash, erasing it from the hard drive. Or maybe I hadn't. Had I been stupid enough to drag it to the trash and then not empty it? It seemed the only possibility. Unless . . .

I looked across the hall to where Rollin was tossing his books into his locker. He slammed the door and headed my way. "Hey, Ken. How goes it?"

"Rollin, were you dumb enough to retype that letter I wrote?"

He looked confused. "What letter?"

"Fritz's letter. You know, Santa's perverted elf."

He grinned. "Oh, yeah. I'd forgotten about him. I wish you'd kept that letter. It was pretty funny."

"Not very. Did you retype it after I dumped it in the trash?"

"No. What's up?"

"I'll tell you in a minute. Did you see me drag it to the trash?"

"Sure. Right after Sarah called you a jerk."

"Did I empty the trash?"

"Yeah, I think so. Come on, what's up?"

I told him. His face got very serious. "You kept me out of it?"

"Yeah, I kept you out of it."

He thought for a long minute. "Who's trying to get you?"

"I don't know. I wish to heck I did."

"Sarah was the only other person to read that letter. And she wouldn't. I mean, why would she be that mad at you?"

"I don't know. But I guess I'd better ask her."

"Norton Utilities," Sarah said.

"Huh?" I said.

She closed the wardrobe closet and sat down at the make-up table. We were backstage, the silence echoing around us. "You can use it to find accidentally trashed files," she said. "When you dump the trash, its contents aren't really erased. All that's erased are the icons and names in the directory window. The documents still exist on the hard drive until they're overwritten. So, somebody could have gone into the hard drive and found your stupid letter with Norton Utilities."

"But who?" I asked.

She shrugged. "Anyone who knows jack about computers. Which you obviously don't."

I thought. And then I had it. "You mean any *nerd*! Rolf Egglehart was in the lab that period. I remember staring him down."

"You're right!" Rollin yelped. "And I saw him down there just a few minutes ago."

"Let's go," I said. "I am going to strangle that kid."

"Now take it easy, Kenny," Sarah said. She paused to lock the stage door before hurrying after us.

Rolf glanced up from his computer screen and then looked at the oversized watch on his skinny wrist. "Thirty-six minutes. Not bad. But then Sarah probably helped you figure it out."

"You nerd!" I snarled. "I'm going—"

"Careful," he said, "I wouldn't make any threats if I were you. Not until you've seen this."

He swiveled the terminal so we could see:

FRITZ THE PERVERTED ELF

BROUGHT TO YOU BY

THAT STAR OF ARGYLE WEST FOOTBALL

KENNETH "THE JERK" BAUER

Hey, Mary,
 I'm Fritz, Santa's perverted elf. I collect little
girls' . . .

Rolf punched a command on the keyboard and leaned back. "In five minutes, that's going to hit the network. Every computer's going to have it by e-mail, and every fax machine and printer in every school building in the system is going to spit out a copy. And none of you, not even Sarah, knows enough to stop it."

My insides went hollow. I stared at him. "What do you want from me?"

"Not a thing. I got what I want. Payback. Big time."

"For what? For a few—"

He was out of his chair, anger suddenly making him look hard, almost vicious. "No, for *a lot* of stupid jokes! For a lot of . . ." He made a gesture like he was wringing the neck of a chicken. "For all the years, for all the gym classes, for every time somebody put me down just because I don't happen to have the genes to be a jock or six-feet tall or handsome enough to get dates with girls like her." He gestured at Sarah. "For all that. Well, this time, *I* win."

I stared at him, openmouthed. "Hey, I never gave you that much trouble. I never—"

He made the neck-wringing gesture again, sat down, and folded his arms.

I slumped in a chair by a laser printer.

"Hey, Rolf," Rollin said. "A lot of that was just teasing. It's not like—"

"Wrong approach," Rolf snapped. "Besides, nobody respects a straight man." He glanced over his shoulder at the timer ticking away in the corner of the computer screen. "Three minutes left. Do you want to give it a shot, Sarah?"

She compressed her lips. "Look, Rolf. I never liked the nerd jokes. They were tasteless, they weren't funny, and I'm sorry you took them so personally. But I don't think they're a big enough reason to destroy Kenny's life. And that's what's going to happen, you know. It's bad enough that McDunn, Mathias, and Wenzel saw that letter, but if everyone sees it . . . Well, it's just going to be awful, Rolf." And to my astonishment, her eyes filled with tears.

"I'm touched," Rolf said. "But, hey, he wrote the letter. And maybe everybody should know what kind of thoughts he can—"

I slammed my fist on the table. "I'm not a pervert! I wrote something stupid, but I would never hurt a kid. Call me anything else you want, but I am no pervert."

Rolf smiled crookedly. "Well, that certainly opens up some interesting possibilities for name-calling. But I'll give you that. I think you're a jerk, but I don't think you'd sexually abuse a kid." He turned to the keyboard. "Well, this isn't getting us anywhere. Let's speed things up."

He hit a couple of keys, the timer went to zero, and I think my heart actually stopped for a second. The laser printer beside me hummed to life, and a sheet slid out. With leaden fingers, I picked it up.

Dear Mr. Wenzel:

I am the one who sent you Fritz the perverted elf's letter. I recovered it from the hard drive of the computer Ken Bauer was using in the lab. I did not find it by accident, but intentionally, using the recovery procedure available with Norton Utilities. I sent it to you not out of a sense of civic duty but to do as much damage to Ken's reputation as I could. I do not regret that. Nor do I apologize for inconveniencing you. I've seen you at every sporting event I've ever attended at Argyle, but not once at a Quiz Bowl or a forensics contest. So, it shouldn't be too hard to figure out exactly what I think your time is worth.

I do not, by the way, think Ken Bauer is a pervert. A jerk and a lot of other things, but I don't think he harms little kids. That, for what it's worth, is my opinion.

The game's over now. I have permanently erased Fritz the perverted elf's letter from the lab computer, which means you have the only remaining copy. Do with it what you like and with this letter also. I could care less.

Sincerely,
Rolf Egglehart

Rolf took the letter from my fingers and scrawled his signature on it. "The Fritz letter didn't go out on the network?" I asked.

"Nope. It's erased, as I said."

"How do I know you don't have a copy somewhere?"

"You don't." He handed the letter back to me.

"What am I supposed to do with this?"

"You can chew it up and choke on it for all I care. But if I were you, I'd give it to Wenzel."

"But he's going to punish you for—"

He laughed, for the first time actually sounding amused. "Well, now I really am touched that you should care. But what can he do to a nerd? Take away my athletic eligibility? Ban me from the computer lab? Suspend me for a few days? I'd like that. I've got a computer at home that can torch anything here. I'd love a few days to work on it."

"How about your folks?" Sarah asked.

He shrugged. "It's just Dad and me. And he's kind of a nerd, too. He'll understand."

"You win," I said.

"Darn right I do," he said, and walked out of the room, his head held high.

I stared at the letter. "You gonna give it to Wenzel?" Rollin asked.

I nodded. "That's what Rolf wants. He wants to stick it to everybody. And some of us just may deserve it."

Rolf's letter didn't solve everything, of course. I'd still written the Fritz letter, and Wenzel, Mathias, and McDunn still thought that was pretty weird. But Rollin and Sarah stood up for me, telling them I was stupid but not dangerous. And I told Mrs. Carruthers everything, because I knew I could count on her to tell them the same thing.

Rolf came out of his interview with Wenzel looking neither shaken nor contrite. The only thing he didn't get was the three days he wanted at home. I guess Wenzel figured it was time that everybody just shut up about the whole thing.

I never got to do another performance of *Santa's Workshop,* but that was a pretty small price to pay.

I said "hi" to Rolf in the halls a few times in the weeks after Christmas vacation, but he ignored me. I let it go for a while, but then I got stubborn and started again. Finally, one day he stopped. "All right! Hello, Ken. Now what do you want?"

I hesitated. "To be friends, I guess."

"Now that is asking a lot. A heck of a lot."

"I kind of think that's what you ask of friends."

He shook his head in frustration. "Why would you want to be friends?"

I shrugged. "I don't know, Rolf. I really don't. It's just that we've been through something together. I had a fight with Rollin in grade school. It was only after that we really got to be friends. We'd been through something together."

"And you think this is an analogous situation?"

"Well, it's sort of the same, anyway."

He sighed. "That's what analogous means. Well, I'm gonna have to think about this." He turned and started down the hall.

"Uh, I'll see you next week," I called after him.

He waved a hand without turning.

"So no more nerd jokes?" Sarah asked.

"Haven't told one in a couple of months. I thought you'd noticed," I said.

"I did, but with you there's always the chance of a relapse."

"No, I'm off nerd jokes for good. Some of the guys I used to call nerds really scare me now. But, hey, did you hear about the blonde who . . ."

"Kenny," she said, "shut up."

And since we spend a lot of time together these days, doing the boyfriend-girlfriend thing, I said, "Yes, ma'am," grinned at her, and leaned in to see if there might just be a quick kiss in it for me. There was.

PIG BRAINS

Featuring:
Don Shadis, *inoffensive person*
Randy "the Doughnut" Schmidtke,
   offensive tackle and person
Melinda Riolo, *former fat person*
Mr. O'Brien, *line coach and hyperactive
   teacher*

I was headed for the main doors and the fall afternoon when a voice behind me boomed, "Hey, Shadis!"

I turned, smile fixed, resigned to taking the usual load of garbage from my favorite Neanderthal: the Doughnut. Now Doughnut's a big guy, about six-four and maybe two-sixty, making him a foot taller and about a hundred and fifty pounds heavier than I am. Fortunately, the brain that knocks around inside his massive skull is inversely proportional to his overall size. Put another way, I'm twice as smart. Which is handy. "Hey, Doughnut," I said.

He flopped a python-thick arm around my shoulders. "When you going out for football, Donny? I could use a blocking dummy." He guffawed. Nitwit.

"Maybe next year," I said, and changed the subject. "What are you bringing to O'Brien's class tomorrow?"

"Huh?" he said.

"Food, Doughnut. We're supposed to bring something that reflects our ethnic heritage." Which in your case would probably be raw mastodon, I thought, but didn't say.

"Oh, yeah," he said, "I nearly forgot. My mom's going to make some doughnuts. We're German, and Germans eat a lot of doughnuts."

"Do they?" I said, to be polite.

"Yeah. At least my family does." He grabbed a fistful of his belly with typical lineman's pride. "Doughnuts put lead in my pants so I can block better. Coach O'Brien loves how I block. And he loves my mom's doughnuts, too."

"Really," I said.

"Yep. I brought six dozen to practice just last week. They were all gone in five minutes."

"Do tell," I said.

"Yep. So who else is bringing food tomorrow?"

"It's you, me, and Melinda Riolo this week."

"Melinda? Hey, you kinda liked her last year, didn't you?"

"She's okay," I said.

"I think she thinks you're a nerd." He laughed.

Well, she thinks you're a baboon! So we're even, jerk. "Makes no difference to me," I said.

He grinned, knowing better. "Yeah, right. So what are you bringing?"

"Brains," I said. "Lithuanians eat a lot of brains."

He stared at me. "You're kidding!"

"Nope. Calf brains, sheep brains, goat brains, all sorts of brains."

He let his arm drop from my shoulder. "That's gross."

"Not really. I like pig brains best. They've got kind of a nutty flavor."

Suddenly his hand was back on my shoulder and it wasn't friendly. He turned me to face him, his eyes mean. "You're putting the Doughnut on, man. I don't like it when people do that. It's like they think I'm stupid or something."

But you are, Doughnut. You are. I just wish you weren't so big. "I'm not putting you on, Doughnut. I swear."

He stared at me for a long minute, his hand slowly

kneading my shoulder. "If you're lying, you'd better tell me now. I might just hurt you a little bit."

I gave the Boy Scout sign. "I swear, Doughnut. I'm bringing Lithuanian fried brains."

He grunted, still looking suspicious, and let me go.

I made it to the street despite wobbly knees and started the walk home past the grade school and down the hill into the Third Ward. What had I done? If I didn't show up tomorrow with Lithuanian fried brains, I'd better show up with a doggone good excuse. Or else Doughnut was going to hurt me a lot more than a little bit.

The logical, really the only noncrazy, thing to do was to come up with a good excuse. But the more I thought about it, the more I really wanted to bring fried brains. I wanted to gross Doughnut out. I mean, the guy grossed me out just by being alive. Now it was my turn.

There really is a recipe for fried brains in the Lithuanian cookbook my mom has. She wrote away for it last spring so she could make a special dinner for my grandpa's eightieth birthday. I helped her pick the menu: "Hey, Mom, here's one we could try. Lithuanian fried brains. Soak the brains overnight in a pan of water in the refrigerator, then—"

"Stop," she said. "I don't want to hear it."

"But, Mom! Maybe Grandpa had them growing up. Maybe he's been longing for some fried brains ever since he left Lithuania."

"Believe me, he hasn't. He's a finicky eater. It drove your grandma nuts."

"Aw, Mom—" I whined.

"No brains! Find something else."

By the time I got home, the sheer brilliance of my inspiration had produced some blind spots in my usually acute vision. Except for twenty or thirty sound, sane reasons, I couldn't see why I shouldn't bring fried brains. Oh, there were a few complications—like where to get the basic ingredient—but that was minor stuff. I could make this happen.

I called Lerner's Meat Market and asked if they had any brains. Mr. Lerner laughed. "No, I haven't seen brains for sale in years. Nobody around here cooks brains. Maybe in Albania or someplace, but not in central Wisconsin."

"Rats," I muttered.

"Nope, we don't have them either. You might try Albertson's Supermarket, though. They might have rats."

"Ha, ha," I said, "very funny."

"We try. What do you want the brains for?"

"A science project."

"Oh. Well, you might try the stockyards over in Stuart."

How was I supposed to get to Stuart without a car, a license, or a gullible parent? (My mom was decidedly ungullible, my dad permanently absent without leave.) "Do you suppose Albertson's might have some brains?" I asked.

"You could ask, but I'd bet a hundred to one against."

"Well, thanks, Mr. Lerner."

"Sure enough. Good luck."

I slumped in the chair. No brains, no gross out of the Doughnut. Rats and double rats. (Or words to that effect.)

But the idea wouldn't go away, and I had my second inspiration of the day. Remember the Halloween game where squealing kids pass the pieces of Frankenstein's monster from hand to hand under a sheet: grapes for the eyeballs, a carrot for the nose, pepper slices for the ears, *spaghetti for the brains*? Shadis, I told myself, you are brilliant.

I peddled my mountain bike down to Albertson's Supermarket and inspected the pasta selections. I finally decided on fettuccine, although I was briefly tempted by some green linguine.

Mom was meeting a client for supper, and my sister was studying at a friend's, so I had the kitchen to myself. Good thing, because making some passable brains out of fettuccine took quite a bit of experimentation. I finally managed what I thought was a pretty good facsimile by cooking the noodles al dente, rolling them in cornmeal, and frying them in some oil. I drained them on paper towels, stuffed them into a loaf pan, and stuck it in the refrigerator.

By then I was on a pretty good roll. A dip, I thought. We need some brain dip. I searched the refrigerator and found half a bottle of cocktail sauce. I poured it into a neutral container and wrote "Lithuanian Brain Dip" on a label. Nah, I could do better than that. I tore it off and wrote "Cozzackakus: Blood of the Cossacks" on a fresh label. Much better.

Digging around in the refrigerator at breakfast the next morning, my sister yelped, "Oh, gross!"

Mom looked over her shoulder. "What on earth?"

"Don't touch," I said. "Social studies project."

"What could this possibly have to do with social studies?" Mom asked.

"Really!" my sister said.

"I meant science," I said. "You don't want to know any more."

"You've got that right," Mom said. "Just get it out of my refrigerator."

By that time the dazzle of my idea had faded considerably, and I was having some decidedly unpleasant second thoughts. Playing a joke on Doughnut was dangerous enough, but getting caught by Mr. O'Brien might be even worse. Mr. O'Brien doesn't fit the stereotype of an assistant football coach. He doesn't have a big belly, he doesn't glower a lot, and he doesn't think football is the most important thing in the world. He thinks social studies is. He expects a lot, even from Doughnut, who sits in the back of the class trying to look interested. (Doughnut thinks O'Brien is God. Or just about.)

Mr. O'Brien pegs the needle on his hyper meter at least four or five times a day. He crashes around the room, slapping his pointer on maps, globes, and time lines. He pounds his fist on his desk, climbs on his chair, role-plays this or that historical figure, even beats his head against the wall if that's what it takes to make a point. In other words, he's a heck of a teacher. But he isn't someone to mess with, and I was beginning to wish I was bringing Lithuanian sponge cake or something. Maybe I'd tell everybody that I'd brought Lithuanian cornmeal-coated fried noodles. Big delicacy, if you're into that kind of thing. Then

I'd lie like crazy to Doughnut and hope he only broke a couple of my bones.

Melinda Riolo didn't bother to go to her desk but marched right to the front of the room with her casserole dish. She stood there, tapping her foot, while Mr. O'Brien finished the roll. He smiled at her. "All right, Miss Riolo, go ahead."

She uncovered the dish and tilted it for everybody to see. "I brought eggplant Parmesan. Since I lost all that extra weight in junior high, I don't eat a lot of the fattening stuff Italians like. I mean all the cheese and stuff. But I make an exception when Mom bakes eggplant Parmesan. Enjoy." She set down the dish and marched to her desk across the aisle from mine. My heart bumped a couple of times with longing.

Doughnut swaggered to the front of the room. He opened a big plastic pail of greasy sugar doughnuts. "They're really good," he said. "My mom fries 'em in lard."

Melinda muttered, "Oh, charming. Now they're an extra five hundred calories each." She eyed me narrowly. "You're being quiet today. Did you forget to bring something?"

"No, I've got it right here in the bag."

"What is it?"

"Brains," I said.

"You're putting me on!"

I looked at her and couldn't lie. "Yeah, but don't tell anybody else. It could cost me about sixteen broken bones."

Doughnut finished describing how he could put away

a dozen doughnuts straight from the boiling deep fryer. "Two dozen if they're small. They don't call me the Doughnut for nothing!" He grinned, using both hands to grab fistfuls of his belly. People laughed, and he swaggered back to his desk.

I took a deep breath, followed it with a short prayer, and stumbled confidently to the front of the class. I whipped the towel from the top of the loaf pan. "Ladies and gentlemen, boys and girls, these are Lithuanian fried brains. They're an old delicacy in traditional Lithuanian homes. When we're up at my grandpa's, we play a lot of pinochle. And while we play, we usually have popcorn, chips, or fried brains."

I prodded at the greasy tangle with a finger. "It's kind of hard to find brains to fry sometimes. Sheep and goat brains are supposed to be the best, but there just aren't many sheep and goats around here. Calf brains are easier to get, and they're really good. But I like pig brains best, and that's what I brought today."

Up to this point, I'd been too nervous to look directly at my classmates. But now I chanced it and was greeted by a lot of open mouths, screwed-up noses, and generally horrified expressions. Doughnut was absolutely gray. Good Lord, they believed me! I took a breath and put the accelerator to the floor. "Now when we get the brains, we soak them overnight in a big pan in the refrigerator. It's kind of a good thing to remember they're in there. Otherwise, the next time you open the refrigerator, it's—whoa—Frankenstein's laboratory! But you kind of get used to that sort of thing around my grandpa's house."

I dug into the tangle, separated a sticky wad of three or four noodles, and held it up. "The next morning we slice the brain and it falls apart into these sort of floppy, wormlike things." (There were some very satisfying groans. Doughnut had gone from gray to ashen.) "We roll them in cornmeal and fry them in oil. We drain them on some paper towels and then put them on the table in a big bowl. Brains are really best served hot, but they're still good cold. Like popcorn's good hot or cold."

I headed the wad of noodles toward my mouth, then pulled it back at the last second. "Whoops, I almost forgot. There's also the dip my mom makes from an old recipe my grandma brought from the old country. It's called *Cozzackakus*, which means 'Blood of the Cossacks.' I asked my grandpa about the name, and he said it's because Lithuanians don't like Cossacks, who used to be these real tough bandit types who raided a lot. My grandpa says not even Cossacks like Cossacks that much, so—"

Mr. O'Brien interrupted. "This would be an example of an ethnic prejudice, class. As we discussed, many older people have them. Go ahead, Don. This is just great."

"Ah, thanks. Anyway, I'm not sure my grandpa ever actually knew any Cossacks, but that's how the sauce got its name. So here's how you eat pig brains." I dipped the noodles in the shrimp sauce, stuck them in my mouth, and chewed. They were terrible, but I grinned. "This is a really good batch. Pig brains are just so much better than calf or beef. Did I mention beef brains? The butchers stopped selling them because people started worrying about mad cow disease. But my grandpa says all Lithuanians are already pretty crazy so they probably wouldn't get any worse if they caught it. So, anyway, who'd like to try some Lithuanian fried brains?"

Nobody moved for a long minute. Then Melinda stood and strode to the front of the class. She gave me a look that was at least half glare. "I bet these are fattening as all get out."

"I don't know, Melinda. Maybe a little."

She plucked a few noodles from the pan, dipped them in the cocktail sauce, and popped them into her mouth. She chewed and then shrugged. "Not bad. Could use some salt, maybe."

Mr. O'Brien jumped up. "Okay, everybody line up. You know the rules: everybody's got to try everything unless you've got a genuine, doctor-certified food allergy." He rubbed his hands together. "This is great! Just great. This is what we want. Something unusual. Something really authentic. Come on, everybody. Line up. Paper plates and spoons are right here. Don and Melinda, go ahead. No standing on ceremony here."

When we were back at our desks, Melinda glared at the doughnut on her plate. "I'd rather have brains." She leaned over and started to whisper. "You were kid—"

"Hold on, Doughnut!" Mr. O'Brien shouted. "You missed the brains. No cheating."

Doughnut grinned sheepishly and dug a few noodles from the pan.

"Don't forget the blood sauce, Doughnut," I called. "Makes them even better."

At his desk Mr. O'Brien was digging into a big serving of brains. He smacked his lips. "You know, Don. If I didn't know better, I'd swear these were noodles."

I almost choked on a bite of eggplant but managed a weak smile. "Yeah, they're kind of similar, aren't they?"

"Sure are. What do you think, Doughnut?"

Doughnut was sitting at his desk, staring at his plate. He looked up pleadingly at Mr. O'Brien, who gave him a now-be-a-man stare. Doughnut sighed, picked up a shred of brains, and stuck it in his mouth. It was a moment of high drama, but I couldn't help glancing at Melinda to see if she was savoring it as much as I was. That's how I missed Doughnut's bolt for the bathroom. He only made it as far as the tall wastebasket beside the door. And when he let go, it was pretty awesome. The metal can resonated like a kettle drum, amplifying the heave into something truly stupendous—a barf worthy of the Doughnut in all his grossness. The sound and the smell set off a chain reaction that sent about ten girls and just as many guys out the door and down the hall to the rest rooms.

Mr. O'Brien stood at the front of the class, hands on hips, glaring at Doughnut's broad rear end as Doughnut heaved a couple more times. He shook his head. "Well, that's it for today, I guess." He waved a hand at the few of us who still sat frozen in our seats. "The rest of you can go. I've got to get Doughnut cleaned up. Don, Melinda, come get your dishes."

I picked up the half-empty loaf pan and followed Melinda out. At the door, I paused. "I'm sorry, Mr. O'Brien."

He slapped me on the shoulder. "Not your fault we've got a bunch of sissies in this class. You did a great job. The most original ethnic dish we've ever had. An A plus all the way. Right, Doughnut?"

Doughnut leaned back on his heels, his face the color of dirty gym socks. "Right, Coach."

"As a matter of fact, we've got a big game Friday night. Maybe I'll have Don bring a couple of pans of brains by the locker room. Some fried brains and some Blood of the Cossacks might be just the thing you boys need to fire up for a game against the conference champions. What do you think, Doughnut?"

Doughnut looked at Mr. O'Brien and then at me. I am dead, I thought. "Right, Coach. I'll do better. I promise. I'll be the first one to take some."

"Darn right you will. Now are you man enough to take that wastebasket down to the custodian's room and wash it out?"

"Yes, sir."

We watched him trudge down the hall, head hanging. Mr. O'Brien slapped me on the shoulder a final time. "Good work, Shadis. See you tomorrow."

A half block from the school, Melinda was sitting on one of the swings in the playground behind the grade school. "Okay," she said. "What were they really?"

"Fettuccine."

"Yeah, I thought so. Did O'Brien catch on?"

I shrugged. "If he did, he decided to go along with the joke."

"You're lucky. You were way out on the edge. What did he say to you?"

"Not much. He said maybe he'd have me bring a couple of pans of brains to the locker room before Friday night's game."

She laughed. "Cool. Half those jocks would lose their lunch. Are you going to do it?"

"Are you kidding? I don't have that kind of death wish. I think pig brains may be real hard to find for the next few weeks."

"And sheep, goat, and calf brains?"

"Them, too," I said.

She laughed again. "I'm glad you did it. Took Doughnut down a notch." She grinned at me. "And put you up a couple, even if nobody but me knows what you really had in that pan."

I shrugged. "That's okay. I don't want to be a dead hero. . . . Hey, you walking my way?"

"Yeah, I could do that," she said. "Definitely."

STORIES FROM
JUNIOR YEAR

BUCK'S HEAD

Featuring:
Ken Bauer, *tight end and co-conspirator*
Rollin Acres, *fullback and lovesick fool*
Sandy Dunes, *goddess in running shorts*

I had a hunch from the first that pairing two names as weird as Rollin Acres and Sandy Dunes might produce some very strange results. I hinted as much to Ramdas Bahave when we saw Rollin and Sandy ahead of us in the hall between fifth and sixth period. "What do you think of the weird-name karma?"

"Ah, my friend," he said, "karma's character is of necessity mysterious or it would not be karma. It is like cement in the hands of the Builder, who of simple bricks makes many wondrous forms."

"What is that supposed to mean?"

"I am not sure. I just made it up. It is worth thinking about, though."

"Right," I said. "But, really, what do you think of those two hooking up? I mean, except for weird names, they have zip in common."

Ramdas smiled. "It does seem an eccentric attraction."

"You got that," I said.

Okay, let's examine these specimens of "eccentric attraction." Rollin could model for a Norman Rockwell calendar: blond, husky, freckles, vaguely goofy grin. On the football field, he's a fullback, accustomed to laying big blocks and eating a lot of dirt. Subtle, he ain't. Off the field, he's as mellow as his name. He gets by in school, works a couple of nights a week unloading trucks for Our Town Foods, sings in the church choir, and generally doesn't get real worked up about much of anything. In short, he ain't a high-energy personality, just a laid back, small-town boy, who would rather mosey than run.

But Sandy has so much energy she sets my teeth on edge. She doesn't walk, she trots, her mouth going all the time. I suppose her dad calls her his Little Pixie or something of the sort. But somehow she misses being Pixie cute. Her features are too sharp, her eyebrows too arched, her eyes too piercing. She's a cross-country runner and a pretty good one. I don't think she's a natural athlete, but she makes up for it with scary competitiveness. This girl will kill herself to finish at the top. But she never quite manages because there's always Kendra Mueller to beat and she can't quite do it.

Personally, I find Sandy exhausting. Oh, I like her well enough. She's funny, kind, interested in other people, and absolutely who she is all the time. But I would never in a million years imagine falling in love with her. But Rollin took a belly flop off the diving board of love on the first day of school. We were sitting in English class, Mr. Franklin calling the roll. Every year teachers react the same way to Rollin's weird name. Mr. Franklin was no exception, hesitating before pronouncing "Rollin Acres?" Rollin waved a hand. Mr. Franklin eyed him. "Interesting name. Did I pronounce it correctly?"

"Yep," Rollin said, "just like a housing development."

"Hmmm . . . There's a word for that sort of name, *euphonic*."

"Oh," Rollin said. "Is that good?"

"Well, it's not really a question of value, just a term for a musical pairing of words."

"Okay," Rollin said. "I get it." Which he didn't, of course, but didn't care.

A few names further on, Mr. F. came to Sandy Dunes. "Yo," she chirped. "I got one of those euphonious names, too."

Mr. Franklin smiled. "You probably want to say euphonic. Less danger of being accused of having an alias or a pseudonym."

"Okeydoke. Euphonic it is."

Okeydoke? Not even my grandpa used that one. I turned in my chair to have a closer look at her. Beside me, Rollin sat mesmerized. "Wow," he breathed. "Sandy Dunes. Isn't that beautiful? Man, I like that."

"She ain't much to look at," I said.

"I like how she looks. I'm going to talk to her after class."

When the bell rang, he managed to intercept her before she galloped off. "Hi," he said. "I'm Rollin Acres."

"Right. With the euphonic name." She stuck out a hand. "Glad to meet ya'. Tell me about yourself. Thirty words or less. I've got to get to the library."

"I'll walk with you."

"Okay."

Under the circumstances, you might think that Sandy would keep her pace to a stroll. Nope, off she charged, Rollin hustling to keep up. I was left behind without even an introduction.

And this is my best friend, Ken Bauer.

Nice to meet you, Sandy.

You, too, Ken. My, you're a big, handsome guy. Smart too, I bet.

(Aw-shucks grin.) Well, I try.

Nope, not so much as a "see you later."

At football practice Rollin was just a blob of lovesick Jell-O oozing around without a care. Not a good attitude when scrimmaging the first-string defense. He got his lunch handed to him about three times in a row. A thorough tongue-lashing from Mr. Hardin, the running backs coach, got his head in the game. But a few plays later the cross-country team ran by, Kendra Mueller leading the pack with her long graceful strides, Sandy hanging doggedly on her heels with her short, choppy ones. Rollin forgot everything, straightening out of his stance a count early to watch. The pass rushers teed off, blasting through the line before the offensive blockers could react. Rollin was still looking the other way when Bill Patchet decked him with a forearm to the chest on his way to sacking the quarterback.

Rollin lay stretched out, gaze fixed dreamily on the high blue sky. I knelt beside him. "Are you alive?" I asked.

"Isn't she beautiful?" he breathed.

Ramdas came jogging up with the medical bag. "Are you badly hurt, Rollin?"

"It's love," I said. "Just shoot him. It'll save us all a lot of trouble."

Sarah joined me when I came out of the locker room. "That was quite a hit Billy Patch laid on Rollin."

"How come you saw that?"

"Didn't you hear the pep band practicing? We were right there in the bleachers."

"Oh, yeah. Right."

"Hmmmph . . . And to think I wasted those fanfares on you. Anyway, what gives with Rollin? He seemed awfully distracted."

"He fell in love with Sandy Dunes today."

"*Sandy Dunes?* You mean we're going to have two kids with names like golf courses going together?"

"If Rollin's got anything to say about it we will. Know her?"

"A little bit. She transferred from East. She used to run cross country there. Kendra Mueller beat her at every meet. Now they're on the same team, I suppose."

"Yep, I saw them practicing today. As a matter of fact, that's what distracted Rollin."

"All you guys ogle the cross-country girls."

"Not me. I've got ogles just for you."

"Yeah, tell me another one."

"Well, I sure don't ogle girls when Billy Patch is rushing the passer. Real bad move."

"Not even me?"

"Not even you. I want to live to ogle another day."

That night Rollin went over to Sandy's house and threw his quivering heart at her feet. (As I said, this guy ain't subtle.) You'd think that such devotion might elicit a response a degree or two above body temperature, but she's been pretty cool toward him. They've gone out a few times in the last six weeks, and she lets him hang around her in school. But Sandy's passion for cross country doesn't seem to leave much room for romance. It's sort of like a person who really doesn't like dogs putting up with a slobbering, worshipful golden retriever while a friend's on vacation. *Okay, Okay. Good dog. I know you love me, but back off! And please roll up your tongue so I'm not slipping on drool all the time.* It's tough on Rollin.

This past Wednesday Sarah and I met Rollin and Sandy for pizza after practice. For once, Sandy was quiet. "What's under your skin?" I asked her.

"Kendra Mueller. You should have seen her this afternoon. I was chugging along with a couple of other girls, just finishing up our five miles, and *zoom,* she sprints past us like she was finishing a fifteen hundred. I know, just absolutely know, that she did it to make us look bad, me especially. *Hey, look at me, Coach! Everybody else is sucking fumes, but I've got lots left in the tank!* Stupid blonde bimbo."

"Doesn't sound much like Kendra," Sarah said.

"Ha! You don't know what she's like out there on the course. She likes to humiliate people. I'd give anything to beat her just once. Here's a little humiliation for you, bimbo-girl."

"Maybe this Saturday . . ." Rollin began and then seemed to think better of it.

"Oh, would I love that," Sandy said. "The Argyle West Invitational, our big home meet. That would be really sweet. Just pray for rain, guys."

"Why's that?" I asked.

"Because I'm best in the rain. Kendra's such a wimp. She hates getting wet and muddy but I could care less. Last week we came to this mud puddle, and she must have wasted ten or fifteen seconds finding a way around it. I just went right through it. But she still caught me with a couple hundred yards to go."

The pizza came and we ate. Sarah took the opportunity to change the subject with a howler about the pep band's demented director. It was a good story, but Sandy was too lost in her own bitter thoughts to even smile. Later, when I said good-bye to Sarah, she gave me a long, steady look. "I know you and Rollin have this blood-brother thing, but don't let him talk you into anything stupid. This is Sandy's problem, and Kendra's our friend, too."

"I know. Don't worry."

"Kenny, I mean it. Rollin's a little crazy right now, and I don't want you two getting into any trouble."

"I promise," I said. And I meant it.

Thursday after practice Coach Carlson sent Rollin and me to Rothburg to pick up some scouting tapes. We did our duty, spent the twenty he'd given us for supper on a couple of subs, and drove back through the Indian summer evening in my modestly disreputable F-150 pickup, the Green Hammer. In my benevolent mood, I tried to cheer Rollin up with a few rousing choruses of "Onward, Green Hammer" sung to the tune of "Onward, Christian Soldiers." But some people you just can't satisfy.

He let out a long sigh. "It doesn't look like it's going to rain."

"Nope, clear all weekend. Good weather for the game."

"I was thinking about the invitational on Saturday."

"You gotta stop worrying about that. Sandy will run a good race. Kendra will run a little better one. I'm sorry, but that's just the way it'll be. . . . By the by, you don't really believe that stuff about Kendra trying to show up Sandy, do you?"

"Why shouldn't I believe it?"

"Because it's not true. Kendra doesn't have a mean bone in her body. She was probably just kicking it in to see what kind of time she could make."

"Yeah, maybe, but I still want Sandy to win. Right now, she's driving me nuts. Cross country this, cross country that. Kendra this, Kendra that. I think if she just won once she'd relax and pay more attention to me."

"No, she wouldn't. She'd just start talking about beating Kendra twice to prove it wasn't a fluke."

"Maybe," he said, "but I'd still like to see her win."

I shrugged. "What's gonna happen is gonna happen. Nothing you can do to change it."

It was then that Rollin saw the dead buck on the shoulder of the road and was struck by inspiration. "Slow down," he said.

"Why?"

"I want to have a closer look."

"It's just a dead deer," I said, but took my foot off the gas.

"Big one. That must be an eight-point rack. Pull over to the side."

"You already had a closer look."

"Come on, man. Gimme a break."

I pulled over, stopping just beyond the carcass. Rollin hopped out. I followed, already suspecting that I was going to regret this.

The buck had been hit a day or two before, and its belly was bloated to twice its normal size. Rollin ignored the stink. He grabbed the buck by its antlers and lifted the head. "Wow, its head is half torn off. He didn't feel much."

"Good. I'm happy for him. Let's go."

"Just a second. I'm thinking."

"Please don't."

"Suppose we put this on the cross-country course on Saturday."

"Yeah, suppose we did. Ha, ha. Funny joke."

"Think about it. Sandy says Kendra's kinda prissy. If she won't run through puddles, just think how she's going to feel about a rotting deer corpse."

"Rollin . . ."

"If we put it in the right place, it'll take Kendra a couple of minutes to find a way around it. But Sandy will jump right over it and keep going. She'll beat her for sure."

"You're nuts," I said. "Besides, I don't want to mess up the race for everybody. Those kids practice just as hard as we do. "

"Why would we be messing up the race? It's cross country. The runners are supposed to expect obstacles: puddles, mud, hills, fallen trees. What's so different about a dead deer?"

"Well . . ."

"Come on, Ken. I've gone along with some pretty goofy stunts of yours. Like when we stole the Bucky Beaver statue over in Montrose just before we played them last year. We could really have gotten into trouble for that."

That we could have. "But Bucky didn't stink," I whined.

"Come on, you wuss. Grab the back legs." I grabbed the back legs, and we heaved the buck into the back of the Hammer.

We hid the carcass next to the service road, a few hundred yards from where the cross-country course runs along the edge of Oakview Park. On the way into town, I tried a final time to talk some sense into Rollin. "Look, this is the last invitational of the year. So what if Sandy doesn't win? She'll get over it and start paying more attention to you."

"There's still sectionals."

"All right, there's still sectionals, but there'll be a couple of dozen schools there. Not the same thing."

"Save your breath. I'm going to do it. If you want to fink out, fine. Just don't expect me to go along with any more of your bright ideas."

But you don't need to do this, Rollin! "Okay," I said. "I'm in. Tell me the plan."

Friday night we squeaked by a good Riter's Point team 14–13. I had three receptions, all solid gains, and Rollin had a half dozen carries, likewise short but solid. The rest of the game we blocked for the glory boys.

Saturday morning dawned bright and cool. So much for any last-minute hopes for rain and an excuse to abandon Rollin's plan. I picked him up at nine and drove down to the park. He was wound up, his nerves making his voice tight. "Okay, we're only going to have twenty minutes, maybe half an hour after the teams finish their practice runs before they line up for the start. We'll drag the deer onto the course maybe ten minutes before the gun and then beat it back to the truck. Plenty of time to get to the starting line."

"Rollin—"

"Don't even start. Remember Bucky Beaver?"

"Yeah, I remember."

"All right then. Now suck it up."

I parked off the service road. Rollin produced a coil of rope. "I brought this so we don't have to touch the buck with our hands."

"Good," I said. "My hands still stink from the last time."

"I never knew you were such a wuss. Come on."

We followed the stench to where the carcass lay in the brush. "Eeeyuck," I said. "Something's been chewing on it."

"Dogs probably. Our Chesapeake is like that: goes out and chews on something dead and then comes home wanting to kiss everybody."

"Charming," I said. "Remind me to get a hamster."

Rollin fastened the rope around the base of the antlers, and we started dragging Mr. Buck through the brush. It was pretty rough going, what with the thickets and gullies. Still, we were making good progress when I heard the first yap behind us. "Did you hear that?"

"Hear what?"

Behind us there was a chorus of yapping, none of it sounding very pleased. "That."

"Just dogs."

"I think they're getting closer."

"Just following the scent. Ignore them."

Easy to say. A minute later, half a dozen dogs burst from the brush behind us, yapping like coyotes on a trail. They were of several different sizes and shapes but apparently all buddies and all intent on the same thing: rotten meat and those who would steal it. They started snapping at the carcass, even grabbing and holding on as we started to run. "Rollin, do something!" I yelled.

"You do something!"

"This is your party, man. You do something."

By now we were dragging not only the deer but three or four dogs. A smallish dog, some kind of miniature collie, started nipping at our heels. Two big mongrels dodged through the brush beside us, barking furiously. "Maybe we ought to give it to them," I yelled.

"No way! Sandy's going to win this race."

A rocky gully opened suddenly in front of us, but we had too much momentum to stop. We plunged over the edge, the carcass and its clinging dogs going momentarily airborne behind us. What came next happened very fast, and I have only a general sense of the sequence. The carcass hit the ground, skidded into a crevice between two rocks on the lip of the gully, and jammed tight. Dogs flew in every direction. I was jerked backward, my feet going out from under me, while Rollin lost his grip on the rope and pitched headlong into the bottom of the gully. I landed flat on my back, the wind whooshing from my lungs.

The abrupt change in our momentum from about fifteen feet per second to zero in the veritable twinkling of an eye tore the buck's head from its mangled neck, launching it in a graceful parabola that I watched with breathless fascination. I wish I could say that I spent the next few moments meditating on the laws of Newtonian physics as applied to the flight of dogs, deer heads, and a couple of really stupid football players. But actually I was trying to remember how to breathe. I eventually got my lungs to work and stumbled to my feet, half expecting to see Rollin lying dead at the bottom of the gully. But one thing you've got to say for the kid: Once he has an idea in his head it ain't easy to knock it out. He staggered up, bruised, scraped, and muddy. "Come on, Ken!" he shouted. "We've still got time. The head will be enough." He grabbed the stinking head by an antler, threw the rope aside, and scrambled up the far side of the gully.

I was still trying to catch up when the screaming started. What the . . . I caught sight of two gray-headed bird-watchers with binoculars fleeing ahead of Rollin. He was brandishing the bloody head by an antler and yelling like a madman for them to let him through.

"Stop!" I shouted. "You're scaring those old ladies to death." I put on a surge of speed and managed to grab him by the back of the belt.

Rollin pulled up, panting hard. "Have to get there. Just a little farther."

I got in front of him, holding up my palms. Somehow we had to get sane again. "No, Rollin, we're cooked. They saw us and they'll talk. Let's just get out of here."

"I gotta do it. Sandy's got to win." Suddenly his eyes opened wide. "Oh, no!"

I looked over my shoulder. The old ladies were coming back, and they had company, as in about six other oldsters, some of whom seemed to be waving stout canes and branches. Rollin dropped the buck's head and ran. I tried to jump over it, caught an antler, sprawled to my hands and knees, and then did a sprinter's start that would have made my coaches proud. We plunged back into the gully and up the other side, passing the pack of dogs tugging and fighting over the buck's carcass. We tore through the thickets, shredding hands and pants, and hit the service road within a few yards of where I'd parked the Hammer. We scrambled in. For a moment I couldn't find my keys and had a terrifying vision of crazed seniors dragging us from the truck to beat and stomp us into a thoroughly tenderized meal for the dogs. "Under the seat," Rollin gasped. "You left them under the seat."

We trudged up the embankment that surrounds the artificial lake at the upper end of the park. Sarah was there in the crowd of spectators waiting for the runners to clear the woods for the final half mile around the pond to the finish line. "Where have you guys been?"

"We got hung up," I said.

She wrinkled her nose. "You smell funny. Sort of a sickly, sweet—"

"I'll shower soon as I can. Just don't ask a lot of questions right now."

She gave me a funny look but turned back to watch as the runners started coming out of the woods. I counted the places. The first eight girls were from other schools, then Kendra came loping into the open, Sandy right on her heels. They climbed the slope, passing a couple of the other girls, to the path running around the lake. I could see Kendra stretching her stride, taking advantage of her long, smooth gait to kick down the next girl in front of her. Behind her, Sandy picked up her own stride. They passed the next girl, leaving only five runners in front of them. Halfway around the lake, Sandy made her move. She pushed up beside Kendra and held there, edging up the pace, trying to break Kendra out of her stride. They passed the next girl without a glance, as if their own duel was all that mattered now. The girl in fourth stumbled, dropping out of their way. But a few paces on, Sandy faltered. I didn't see it at first, but Sarah said, "Uh oh," and

Rollin cursed under his breath. Then Sandy was dropping back, the space between her and Kendra opening rapidly. Rollin turned away.

"Cheer, Rollin," Sarah said quietly. "Cheer her all the way in. That's what you're here for."

"Yeah," I said. "Me, too." And the three of us started cheering not only Sandy but all the girls as they pushed down the last hundred yards to the finish. Kendra finished third, just edging ahead of a skinny redhead from Montrose. Sandy finished sixth, having lost one of the places she'd gained in her duel with Kendra. For a few minutes they walked about, hands on hips, catching their breath.

"Great race, Sandy," Rollin yelled.

She grinned at him, looking positively ebullient. She went over to Kendra and threw her arms around her. Arm and arm they went to the timekeeper's table to check their times. Then they hugged again and actually started jumping up and down. After a minute or two of joyful screaming, they came over to us. Kendra tousled Sandy's short, curly hair. "My rabbit," she said. "Pushed me all the way."

"We both had our best times ever," Sandy said. "Me pushing her, her pulling me. We're a team."

"Here are my folks," Kendra said. "I'll see you guys later." She gave Sandy another hug and jogged off.

"I gotta go, too," Sarah said. "Pick me up at seven, Kenny."

Sandy got her sweats on, and we headed for the Hammer. "Correct me if I'm wrong," Rollin said, "but weren't you guys worst enemies the other day?"

"Me and Kendra? Nah, she's my bud."

"But you said you'd do anything to beat her."

"And I would. But it's not going to happen. I can't match those long legs with my stumpy ones. She's always going to win, but pushing her hard makes me a better runner."

Rollin's voice took on a plaintive edge. "But you were mad as all get out at her. You called her a stupid blonde bimbo."

"Oh, I didn't mean anything by that. I was just psyching myself up for the race. Just a second, I gotta say something to Coach."

Rollin and I stood by the Hammer. "You know something," Rollin said. "I really don't understand girls."

"Join the club," I said.

Sandy came back and we climbed in. She wrinkled her nose. "Something smells awful. What have you been carrying in this truck?"

I glanced at Rollin. "It's a very long story."

"Yeah," Rollin said, "and one maybe we'll skip for right now. Tell us about the race."

She laid her skinny arms across our shoulders. "Well, the woods part was pretty ordinary until we came up on this bunch of old people with binoculars and bird books. Boy, were they mad about something. . . ."

sATYAGRAHA

Featuring:
Ken Bauer, *tight end and blocking dummy*
Ramdas Bahave, *pacifist and trainer*
Bill Patchet, *defensive end and bad attitude personified*

Ramdas Bahave met me at the sidelines. "In what part of the body are you wounded, Kenneth?" he asked.

"Hand," I said, gritting my teeth.

"The smallest finger again?"

"Yeah."

"Let me see it, please."

I held out my right hand, the dislocated little finger already twice its normal size and rapidly turning purple.

Rollin made a barfing sound. "I wish you'd stop messing up that finger, Ken. It's disgusting."

"Just watch the game, Rollin."

"Sure. But, you know, if you had a little more vertical you could catch a pass like that."

"I've got more vertical than you do, jerk."

"You're supposed to. You're a tight end. Who ever heard of a fullback with vertical leap?"

Ramdas interrupted. "Would you like me to correct this problem now?"

"Yeah, do it," I said.

Ramdas took my pinkie in his strong, slender fingers and pulled. Pain shot up my arm and my eyes teared. Dang! This time he really was going to pull it out by the roots. Then there was a pop and a sudden easing of the pain. He felt gently along the joint. "It is back in place. Are you all right? Feel faint, perhaps?"

"I'm OK. Just tape me up and get me back in."

He made a disapproving sound but started buddy-taping my pinkie and ring finger. Out on the field we'd covered the punt and held Slayton High to four yards on two running plays. Still time to win if we could hold them on third down. "Come on, Patch," I yelled. "Now's the time."

"Please hold your hand still, Kenneth," Ramdas said.

The Slayton quarterback dropped back to pass as Bill Patchet, our all-conference defensive end, bull-rushed their left tackle. Bill slung the kid aside, leaped a shot at his ankles by the fullback, and buried the quarterback. The ball popped loose and Bill dove on it, but the ref signaled no fumble, down by contact. Bill jumped up and started yelling at the ref, but a couple of the other seniors pulled him away before he got a flag.

Ramdas handed me a bag of ice. "Here. Sit down. Rest."

"I can't sit down. We're getting the ball back."

While Slayton set up to punt, Coach Carlson strolled down the line to me. "Finger again?"

"Yes, sir."

"Can you play?"

"Yes, sir."

Coach looked at Ramdas, who shrugged. "It is a dislocation like the other times. I think he should keep ice on it."

Coach looked at me. "Right hand?"

I nodded.

"Hard for you to hold onto a football then. I'll put in Masanz."

So that was it for me for that game. We got the ball back on our thirty with two minutes to go. Catman got two quick completions against their prevent defense but couldn't connect on the big pass downfield. Final score: 16–10. Yet another loss for ol' Argyle West.

Bill Patchet spent his usual five minutes bashing his fists, forearms, and head into lockers. At six-four, two-forty, that's a lot of frustration on the loose, and the rest of us stayed out of his way. "Hey, Bauer," he yelled at me. "Where were you on that last series?"

I held up my bandaged hand. "Dislocated a finger."

"And so little doc Ramdas wouldn't let you play, huh?"

"It wasn't like that, Bill."

He didn't listen. Instead he grabbed a roll of tape and fired it at Ramdas, who was straightening up the training room, his back to us. The roll of tape flew through the open door and did a three-cushion bank shot around the room. Ramdas jumped out of the way and looked at us in confusion.

"Hey, Ram!" Bill yelled. "Your job is to get people back in, not keep them out!"

Ramdas didn't answer, only stared. That only made Bill madder, and he started for the door, fists balled. "The idea is to win, you jerk! No matter what it costs. So unless a guy's got an arm ripped off, you get him back in!"

Rollin stepped in front of him. "Come on, Bill. We all feel like crap about losing. You played—"

"He doesn't feel like crap! He doesn't care one way or the other as long as he gets to play with his bandages and his ice bags."

"Yeah, yeah, sure, Bill," Rollin said. "Just let it alone now. Go take a shower. You'll feel better."

Bill stalked back to his corner, smashed another locker door, and started pulling off his uniform.

I got into the passenger seat of Sarah's Toyota. "Tough loss," she said.

"Aren't they all? A couple more, and we'll have to start replacing lockers."

"Billy Patch took it out on poor, defenseless inanimate objects again, huh?"

"Yep. He got after Ramdas, too. Rollin broke it up."

"What's Bill's problem? It's not Ramdas's fault you guys lost."

"Well, Ramdas would rather sit a guy down than risk making an injury worse. Bill doesn't think that's the way to win football games."

Sarah snorted. "So he thinks you should risk permanent injury just to win a stupid game?"

"Something like that. Let's go to Mac's. I'm hungry." I started fiddling with the radio dial, hoping she'd let the subject drop.

She didn't, which is pretty typical of her. "I still don't get it. There's got to be more to it than that."

I sighed. How to explain? "Ramdas doesn't seem to care if we win or lose. And that drives Bill nuts. I mean, look at it from his standpoint. Here he is, the best player on a lousy team. He's been all-conference, but he could have been all-state if he'd played for a winning program. And all-state means a scholarship and the chance to play for a Division One or a Division Two school. All-conference doesn't guarantee anything."

"None of that justifies being mean to Ramdas."

"No, but it explains it a little."

She harrumphed, unimpressed. "So what's going to happen next? Is Bill going to start punching him?"

"I don't think it'll come to that."

"Well, I think it might! And I think you'd better do something about it, *team captain.*"

"Only one of four."

"Still—"

"I know, I know. I'll keep an eye on things."

She glared at me. "You should do a heck of a lot more than that, Kenny."

Maybe she was right, but I didn't plan on doing anything. If Ramdas felt there was a big problem, he should go to Coach Carlson. Me, I was going to ignore the whole thing as long as possible.

We didn't have practice Monday, and I didn't see anything of Ramdas or Bill until Tuesday morning. Rollin and I were coming down the east corridor maybe twenty feet behind Bill when Ramdas turned the corner. Bill took a step to his left and put a shoulder into him. Ramdas bounced off the lockers, skidded on the slippery floor, and only just managed to keep his balance. Bill didn't even look back.

"Uh-oh," I said. "I hope Bill doesn't make a habit of that."

"He already has," Rollin said. "Started yesterday morning. Every time he sees Ramdas, *wham,* into the lockers."

"Wow, did you say anything to him?"

"To Bill?"

"Yeah."

"I said something. Asked him why. He says he's gonna get Ramdas's attention one way or another."

"I don't think getting his attention is the problem."

"Neither do I, but are you going to argue with someone as big and ornery as Billy Patch?"

No, and it wouldn't do any good if I did. Besides, I had a couple of questions of my own for Ramdas.

At noon I found him sitting by himself in the cafeteria, a textbook open beside his tray. I sat down across from him. "Hey, Ram," I said.

"Hello, Kenneth." He marked his place, closed the book, and looked at me expectantly.

"Why do you always use people's full names?"

He smiled and shrugged slightly. "I like their sound. I do not like to use contractions either. I like the full words."

"It makes you sound like a professor or something."

"Sorry."

"Uh, well, not a problem. But, look, you've got to do something about this thing between you and Bill Patchet."

"What would you suggest?"

"For starters you could act like you care if the team wins or loses."

"But I do not care. Football is a lot of pointless violence as far as I can see."

"Then why'd you volunteer to be a trainer?"

"To help with the wounded."

I shook my head. "Well, maybe you could at least stop being so passive about everything."

He laughed. "You would have me fight William Patchet?"

"Well, not exactly, but—"

"Because I will not fight. It goes against everything I believe."

"I don't expect you to fight him, but you can stand up to him in other ways."

"But I am."

"How's that?"

"By not reacting with force. Force is never justified."

"Well, maybe not in this case, but—"

"No, Kenneth, in all cases. Never, no matter how good the cause."

"Oh, come on. How else are we supposed to keep other people or other countries from taking what's ours? Sometimes you've got to use force."

He sighed. "I guess that is what a lot of you Americans believe. But I believe that you can resist in another way. Mahatma Gandhi called it *satyagraha,* to stand firmly for truth and love without ever resorting to force."

I stared at him in disbelief. I mean, Bill was about to turn him into a smear of jelly, and Ramdas was talking about some dead holy man! "Well, that may be very cool, Ram, but—"

"You have heard of Gandhi, have you not?"

"Sure. I mean, the name, anyway. And I'd love to hear more. But right now I think you'd better tell me what you're planning to do about Bill Patchet."

"I am telling you. The Mahatma used satyagraha to free all of India from the British. I think I can use it to control Mr. William Patchet."

Oh, sure. But I bet Gandhi never had to face down six feet four inches and two hundred forty pounds of crazed defensive end. "Ram, listen—"

He interrupted gently. "Let me tell you a story. Under British rule it was illegal for Indians to make their own salt. Everyone had to buy expensive government salt, and that was very hard on the poor. Three thousand of the Mahatma's followers went to protest the law at a place called the Dharasana Salt Works. They stepped four at a time up to a line of soldiers, never lifting a hand to defend themselves, and let the soldiers beat them down with bamboo clubs. Those who could, got up and went to the back of the line. All day they marched up to the soldiers until the soldiers were so tired they could no longer lift their arms."

"What did that prove?"

"It proved that the Mahatma's followers were willing to suffer for what they believed without doing harm to others. Their example brought hundreds of thousands of new recruits to the struggle for independence. Eventually, the jails were full, the country did not work anymore, and the British had to leave."

It was my turn to sigh, because this had gotten a long

way from football or figuring out a way to keep Bill from turning Ramdas into an ooze of pink on a locker door. "Look, Ramdas, that might have worked in India, but in this country—"

"Your Martin Luther King made it work in this country."

"Okay, point taken, but what are you going to do about Bill?"

"Just what I am doing. I am going to answer his violence with satyagraha. Someday, his arms will get tired."

"If he doesn't kill you first."

Ramdas smiled faintly. "There is always a risk."

Ramdas didn't get it. Okay, he was Indian, had moved here with his family only a couple of years ago. But somehow he must have gotten this satyagraha thing wrong. No way could it work. During study hall I went to the library, figuring I could find something that would prove it to him. All the Internet computers were being used, so I went to the shelves. I found a thick book with a lot of photographs of Gandhi and sat down to page through it. And . . . it . . . blew . . . me . . . away. Here was this skinny little guy with thick glasses and big ears wandering around in sandals and a loincloth, and he'd won! And I mean big time: freed his country without ever lifting his hand against anybody. Incredible.

Now, I'm not the kind who tosses and turns half the night worrying about things. I'm a jock. I need my sleep. When I hit the pillow, *bam,* I'm gone. But that night I lay thinking until well past midnight. Hadn't Jesus said to turn the other cheek? Ramdas, who was a Hindu or something, was living that, while most of the guys I saw in church on Sunday would prefer to beat the other guy to a pulp. Man, oh, man, I didn't need this. Let Sarah and Ramdas talk philosophy; I was just a jock. But like it or not, I was going to have to do something or feel like a hypocrite forever.

Wednesday morning I went to see Coach Carlson with my plan. He didn't like it. "Look, I'll get Patchet's attention," he said. "I'll tell him to quit giving Ramdas a hard time."

"Coach, I really want to do this. For a lot of reasons."

We talked some more and he finally agreed, though he still didn't like it much.

Next I talked to Rollin. He shook his head. "Man, you could get hurt. And I mean *bad*."

"I'll take that chance. Just tell the other guys not to step in. And if Ramdas starts to, you stop him."

Finally, I told Sarah. She studied me for a long minute. "You're not really doing this for Ramdas, are you?"

"I'm not sure."

"Can I shoot Bill with a tranquilizer dart if things get out of hand?"

"I guess that wouldn't be too bad an idea. But I don't think they will. He's big, but I'm pretty big, too."

Bill Patchet takes everything seriously, which makes it all the scarier practicing against him. Bill is, by the way, not a dope. He maintains a four-point with a full load of honors classes and is the only kid in school with the guts to carry a briefcase. On the football field, he studies an opponent, figures out his moves, and then pancakes him or blows by him. Believe me, I know; I've been practicing against him for years. But as I'd reminded Sarah, I'm big, too, and I'd seen all his moves.

After drills, the starting teams lined up for a scrimmage. The center hiked the ball to Catman, who was back in the shotgun. Billy hit me with a straight bullrush. I took it, letting him run over me. When I got up and took my stance for the next play, he gave me a funny look. "Ready this time?"

"Yep," I said, and set my feet to make it just as hard as possible for him.

Catman yelled, "Hut, hut, *hut!*" and there was the familiar crash of helmets and shoulder pads. Bill hit me so hard my teeth rattled. Every instinct told me to bring up my arms to defend myself, but I just took the hit. I landed flat on my back, the air whooshing out of my lungs.

He glared down at me. "C'mon, Bauer. Get with the program, huh?"

He must have figured I was trying to sucker him, because the third time he took a step to his right, as if he expected me to come at him hard. Instead, I took a step to my left and let him run me down.

After that play he didn't talk and he didn't try to go around me. He just came at me as hard as he could. After a while the other players stopped practicing and just watched. Catman would yell, "Hut, hut, *hut!*" and the same thing would happen again.

I lost count how many times Bill decked me. Finally, he hit me so hard my ears rang and the back of my helmet bounced two or three times on the turf. I just lay there, too stunned to move, as he stalked off toward the locker room. But it wasn't quite enough. Not yet.

Somehow I managed to stumble to my feet. "Hey, Bill! I can still stand, Bill. Can still stand up to you." He turned and came at me with a roar. And it was the hardest thing I'd ever done in my life to take that hit without trying to protect myself. He hit me with every ounce of his 240 pounds, driving me into the turf, and the world flashed black and then back to light.

We lay a yard apart, panting. "Okay," he gasped. "I give up. What's this all about?"

"It's about standing up without fighting back."

"Don't give me puzzles, man. I'm too tired."

"It's about Ramdas. He doesn't want to fight."

"The little weasel should stand up for himself."

"He is, just like I did now. He calls it satyagraha. I don't know if I'm even pronouncing it right, but it means standing firm without using force. He won't fight no matter what you do."

"That's dumb."

"It's what he believes. I think he's got a right to that."

We sat up, still breathing hard. Bill took off his helmet and wiped sweat from his face. "You were driving me crazy. This was harder than a game. I'm whipped."

I took a breath. "Ramdas told me a story." I told him about the three thousand people who'd walked up to the soldiers at the Dharasana Salt Works and let themselves get beaten down with clubs.

Bill listened. "And that worked, huh?"

"Yeah, it did."

He shook his head. "I couldn't do that. I don't have the guts." He struggled to his feet and plodded toward the sidelines where Sarah, Rollin, Coach Carlson, and most of the team were watching.

I'd lost a shoe in the last collision and spent a moment getting it back on. I looked up to see Ramdas, medical bag over his shoulder, step out from the sidelines to meet Bill. "Are you injured, William?"

Bill stared down at him for a long moment. "Nah, I'm okay." He hesitated, and I could guess how hard it was for him to say more. "But thanks for asking, man." He walked on, head bowed, toward the locker room, the crowd parting to let him pass.

Ramdas came over to me. "And in what part of the body might you be wounded, Kenneth?"

"All over but nothing special."

"Your hand. It is all right?"

"Fine."

He hesitated. "And your spirit? How is it?"

I looked at him, saw his eyes shining with something that might have been laughter or maybe a joy I didn't quite understand but thought I recognized from the old black-and-white pictures of Gandhi and his followers.

"Feeling not too bad," I said. "Not bad at all."

ELVIS

Featuring:

Ken Bauer, *tight end and defender of the downtrodden*

Nancy Iverson, *raven-haired Latina beauty*

Bill Patchet, *defensive end and scary person*

Marvin "the Catman" Katt, *quarterback and irredeemable jerk*

I was bent over the test, trying to translate a paragraph into Spanish, when my pen crashed. I shook it desperately, hoping to reboot. In the desk behind me, Nancy Iverson—who'd finished ten minutes earlier, of course—tested a pen on the back of her paper and handed it to me. "Here, Ken."

I nearly said, "Thanks, Elvis," before catching myself and saying, "Thanks, Nancy."

She smiled slightly and glanced at my paper. "By the way, the word you're looking for is *despertarse*."

Outside in the hall, I said, "Thanks. I couldn't think of that word to save my butt."

She shrugged. "No problem. It's been a while since we learned it."

We walked toward the cafeteria. If any of the football team saw us together, I'd get some crap later. *Hey, saw you walkin' with Elvis. You guys got something hot goin'?* But I try not to let stuff like that bother me. Besides, I've always genuinely liked Nancy. As a friend, that is.

I guess I've got to explain the Elvis thing. Nancy is a big girl, built kind of like a linebacker. And she looks a little like Elvis after he got old and fat. It's the sideburns. Oh, they aren't as long as Elvis's were, but they stand out. She fusses with her hair trying to hide them, but everybody notices. But don't call her Elvis to her face. She will haul off and paste you one. Guaranteed.

"So how come you're so good at Spanish?" I asked. "Do you speak it at home?"

"Oh. Like Iverson's a Spanish name."

"Well, no, but you look—"

"Like a raven-haired Latina beauty?"

"Come on, Nancy. You don't have to be that way with me."

She glanced sideways at me. "Sorry, I forget that some people actually treat me decent. Sarcasm's my natural response to everything."

I didn't comment.

She sighed. "I'm Cuban and Mexican, but I never knew my birth parents. The Iversons adopted me. They didn't speak a word of Spanish as far as I remember. I've been in foster care since I was eight."

"What happened to the Iversons?"

"I don't know. Probably killed each other or drank themselves to death. They weren't exactly a roaring success as parents."

"Tough," I said.

She hesitated. "Yeah, well. Sometimes it goes that way, I guess. . . . Here are my guys, I'll see you later." She broke off to join a knot of Latino kids.

"I've got your pen," I called after her.

"Keep it," she said. "It'll get you through the day anyway."

I sat down next to Sarah at our usual cafeteria table. "So," she said, "I heard you were getting chummy with Nancy Iverson."

"Wow, that didn't take long to spread." I grinned. "Why? Jealous of Elvis?"

"Don't call her that."

"You know I don't. So you're jealous?"

"Nope. Just wondered what you guys were talking about."

"Nothing much. Spanish mostly. She is really good at it."

"Did she tell you that one of the Sanchez brothers is taking her to Homecoming?"

"No foolin'. How do you know that?"

"I was picking up my dress last night, and Nancy was there getting hers fitted. She was embarrassed. Asked me not to tell anybody yet. So don't you go spreading it around."

"Not me. I'm happy for her."

"Me, too. She looked nice." At that I must have looked skeptical, because Sarah suddenly got snappish. "Well, she did, Kenny. Really, really nice."

I held up my hands, palms out to ward off any blows. Why did girls get this way? "Hey, I thought I was one of the good guys here."

She glared at me, lips tight, and then sighed. "Oh, I know you are. It's just that guys can be such jerks sometimes. You know, expecting every girl to be gorgeous."

Well, just call it a marked preference, I thought, but sure as heck didn't say.

Nancy and half a dozen Latino kids came in and started for the far cafeteria line, passing the table where Catman held court among various jocks, their girls, and assorted groupies. Someone shouted, "One, two, three—" And the whole table burst into "Jailhouse Rock." It was a pretty weak performance, nobody really knowing a song that old. But they knew enough to get the point across. Nancy turned and stared, and she didn't look tough or mean, just shocked and more hurt than I thought it was possible for a human being to look. By then everybody in the cafeteria was laughing.

And Nancy ran, out the side door and across the parking lot.

"Oh, God," Sarah breathed. "Somebody ought to go after her."

"I think they're handling it." A couple of teachers descended on the table of aspiring rock singers and started laying into them big time. Mrs. Rove, one of the gym teachers, hurried out the door after Nancy. But I don't think Nancy was waiting around for sympathy.

As I'd predicted, I started getting gas about Elvis as soon as I walked into the locker room that afternoon. "Hey, Bauer," the Catman shouted. "How's it feel to nuzzle up to those sideburns?"

Now I'm a big guy, and I don't have the longest fuse in the world. But before I could rip into Catman, Bill Patchet glared at him. "Why don't you concentrate on practice so we don't get our butts kicked again this week?"

Catman smirked and shrugged, but he didn't give me any more crap. Nobody ignores Billy Patch.

We started drills with Jim Braehm, our number two quarterback, calling the signals. Over on the sidelines, Coach Carlson was chewing out Catman. Bill lined up across from me. "Hey, Bauer."

"Hey, Bill. How you doing?"

"Good. When the Catman comes in, let me know when you're going out on a pattern. I'm going to deck that kid."

"You'll get in trouble. He's got on a no-contact jersey."

"I give a rat's butt. He's got it coming."

"What's up?"

"He bothers me."

"Oh," I said.

Jim Braehm shouted "Hut, hut, *hut!*" and Bill hit me like a locomotive.

After half a dozen reps of the drill, Catman relieved Jim. "I'm releasing into the flat," I muttered to Bill. "Now don't kill him. We've got a game to play Friday."

Bill nodded. I glanced at Saul Goodman, the left out-side linebacker who'd cover me in the flat. Catman shouted: "Seventy-seven, twenty-four, hut, hut—"

Catman got the ball and dropped back looking my way as I ducked past Bill's shoulder and sprinted into the flat, Saul on my shoulder. I looked back for the pass in time to see Bill run Rollin and nail Catman square in the chest with a shoulder pad. "Ouch!" Saul said. "Man, what got into Billy Patch?"

I shrugged and jogged back to our side of the line. Ramdas and a couple of coaches were down beside Cat-man, checking for broken ribs and ruptured internal or-gans. Coach Carlson was screaming at Bill, who stared down at him impassively. I felt a little bad for Rollin, who was stumbling around like he'd had a close encounter with a bus. Catman got up eventually, and we went back to work.

That was about all the excitement for Tuesday and Wednesday of that week. Nancy was back in school, looking grim but in control. Once when I passed her locker, I spotted a couple of Elvis caricatures taped to the door. I ripped them off and crumpled them up, not caring who noticed.

The second I got into Sarah's car Thursday morning, I could tell she was upset. And angry. "She's not going."

"Who? Going where?"

"Nancy's not going to Homecoming. She says Eduardo doesn't have the money for a tux or flowers and stuff. She says all the Latino kids are thinking of skipping the dance."

"Why?"

"They're afraid there's going to be trouble."

"Well, you can tell them for me that there isn't going to be any. *Nada*. Rollin and I will see to that."

She thought for a minute. "But Eduardo's still not going to have the money."

"Well, I don't know that I can help with that. I sure don't have it."

"Maybe we could take up a collection."

I shook my head. "For Elvis to go to the dance? You're kidding."

"We won't say what it's for. We'll just tell people it's a good cause."

I was skeptical. "I don't—"

"Come on, Kenny. You see what you can shake out of the team. I'll go after the *Purple Cow* and drama kids."

"Without telling them what it's for?"

"Right. A charitable cause doesn't always have to be named, does it?"

"Well, maybe you're more persuasive than I am, but—"

"*Kenny*," she said, a hint of warning in her tone.

"Okay, okay," I said. "I'll give it a try."

I felt more than a bit like a fool when I got up with an empty coffee can in my hands and asked the guys to contribute to an anonymous cause. But I gave it my best shot.

"So we're not even supposed to know what it's for?" Saul asked.

"That's right. This time you've just got to trust that it'll do a lot of good."

"What keeps you from ripping us off?" Catman asked.

"I've explained everything to Coach Carlson. He'll make sure the money goes to the right place."

Still, nobody contributed anything but grumbles and whines until Bill Patchet stood up—all 6 feet 4 inches, 240 pounds of him, butt naked and scary. "Come on, you cheap jerks! If Bauer says it's for a good cause, it's for a good cause." He dropped a ten dollar bill into the can and strode toward the showers.

Rollin and I took tens out of our wallets and put them in. Then I handed the can to Saul, who shrugged and tossed in a five. The can went around, some of the guys kicking in, more of them passing it on without saying anything. Catman dropped in a nickel, sneered at me, and headed for the showers. Jerk.

Rollin and I counted the money in the coaches' office. "How'd we do?" he asked.

"Ninety-five oh five. Better than I expected."

"Me, too. And you really won't tell me what this is about?"

"Nope. You've got to trust me just like everybody else."

Coach Carlson came in. "Here, from the coaches." He handed me a small wad of bills. I counted. "That's another forty-five. So one forty-oh-five total."

"Real good," Rollin said.

I saw Bill out in the parking lot. "Thanks, man," I said. "I don't think I would have raised a nickel without you starting it off."

"No problem. Nancy deserves a break."

"You figured it out, huh?"

"It wasn't exactly tough. I saw you tear those pictures off her locker."

"If you don't mind me asking, Bill, why do you care if Nancy goes to the dance or not?"

He shrugged. "I see her at church every Sunday. She kneels there, her eyes closed, praying. And I think, what the heck is she praying for? Is God going to make her better looking? Is he going to give her a couple of parents? Is he going to make people stop picking on her? He didn't exactly give her a lot of breaks. Well, I may not be God, but I can cut her a little slack."

"Oh," I said. "Well, thanks for starting—"

"Forget it," he said. "I'll see you tomorrow."

Sarah had done even better than I had. In the car we counted up a total of $318.05. "Who was the jerk who tossed in a nickel?" she asked.

"Catman."

"Figures. Well, I talked with Mrs. Carlson. She's going to give the money to Eduardo. He might be too proud to accept it from one of us. But she's his counselor, and I think she can convince him it's no disgrace. She's also going to talk to Nancy."

"She's the right choice. I had to fill in Coach Carlson to get permission to ask the guys for money. He promised to keep it quiet. The coaches kicked in forty-five bucks."

"Good." She started climbing out of the car. "I'm going to run this up to the office. Mrs. Carlson said she'd keep it open until I got there. You can think about how you and Rollin are going to get Eduardo fitted for his tux."

"Wait a second. That wasn't part of the deal. He's got friends. Besides, he'd guess we were involved in getting the money together."

She paused, then leaned into the car and gave me a quick kiss. "For once, you're right."

We played Rhinelander Saturday afternoon. Catman was sharp; Rollin and the other running backs got nearly two hundred yards, and yours truly caught four passes, including a touchdown. Meanwhile, Bill had the defense fired up—or else just scared to death. Billy Patch wasn't about to lose his final Homecoming game, and God help anyone who missed a tackle this year. The result was a very satisfying 24-10 win, our best game of the year.

We got to the dance about 8:30 P.M. Sarah looked fantastic. Nearly all the girls did. Even Nancy. (Well, maybe not fantastic, but she looked, to borrow Sarah's phrase, "really nice.") Eduardo, who at maybe five-four was a good six inches shorter than Nancy, looked like he was going to bust out of his tux with pride.

Apparently the word was out that there wasn't going to be any trouble tonight, because Nancy and the other Latino kids were having a blast. About halfway through the dance, the DJ shouted, "Switch up, people. You can't dance with the same person all night."

"I've got Sarah," Rollin yelled, grabbing her hand.

"Watch yourself," I said. "Sarah, if he makes a false move, punch him."

"But suppose I like it?" She grinned, and they headed for the dance floor. I turned, expecting to find Sandy Dunes, Rollin's date, waiting for me. But she was headed off with some sophomore.

I glanced around to see if I could snare another girl. Nancy stood alone, watching Eduardo dancing with a girl I didn't recognize. On impulse, I walked over to her. She looked startled when I held out an arm, but managed a smile and took it.

"How you doin'?" I asked when we were out on the floor.

"Pretty good. Real good, as a matter of fact. How about you?"

"Great. Good game, good dance."

"You were behind the money Mrs. Carlson gave Eduardo, weren't you?"

I hesitated. "Me and Sarah, but a lot of people kicked in. We didn't tell them what it was for. Bill Patchet knows, and I suppose Rollin and Sandy figured it out. Otherwise, it's just Coach and Mrs. Carlson as far as I know."

She nodded. "Well, thanks. This evening was kind of important to us. To me, anyway."

"No problem."

"But I gotta ask. Why are you dancing with me now?"

"Nobody else asked you."

"You know this Elvis garbage isn't going away. You'll get some crap about it."

"I know."

"Then why? And don't tell me just because you felt like it."

I didn't really have an answer for her. "I guess I just don't like other people telling me who I can like."

She leaned back a little so she could look into my eyes. "My God, you're brave."

"Not as brave as you are," I said. "Maybe that's why I'm dancing with you. I'm just hoping some of it will rub off."

"I'm not brave," she said. "I'm scared and sad most of the time."

"You came back to school after that 'Jailhouse Rock' thing. I don't know that I would have."

She didn't say anything, but for a brief moment she laid her head on my chest.

The song ended and we stepped apart. She squeezed my arm. "Thanks, Ken Bauer, you are one good guy."

"You're welcome," I said. "Have a good time tonight."

She grinned. "Oh, I'm gonna. Just wait about five minutes and you'll see just how good a time." She headed back toward the Latino kids, who seemed to be milling about in some excitement.

I rejoined Sarah, Rollin, and Sandy. "Something's about to happen," I said. "I just hope nobody does—"

"Look," Sandy said, "We've got a new DJ."

Sure enough, a Latino guy had replaced the other guy at the controls. *"Muchachos, bailamos la salsa!"* he shouted. Music boomed from the speakers.

"What the heck is that?" Rollin asked.

"Salsa music," Sarah said. "Where have you been?"

"Not listening to that."

The Latino kids streamed onto the floor. And they'd practiced. Nancy, Eduardo, and all of them were whirling and stepping and just putting to shame all the dancing that had come before. Around us there was mostly silence, a few people muttering unhappily. Then Catman and three of his buds stepped from the crowd and started for the DJ. I tensed, and Rollin stepped up beside me. This could get ugly. But they didn't make it halfway to us before they met up with Billy Patch. The song ended just then and everyone could hear what was being said.

"Get out of the way, Bill," Catman said. "We're just going to find out who's behind this."

"And then what?"

"Well, it's our dance. There are more of us than there are of them."

"It's their dance, too."

"Bill, darn it—"

Bill's arm came up then, his big hand moving almost in slow motion toward Catman's face. Almost gently, he put a forefinger to Catman's lips. It was just about the scariest thing I'd ever seen. "Just shut up, Catman. Take your buddies and go on back. People are trying to dance here."

And Catman and his buds turned around. That broke the spell, and the music started again. Bill extended an arm to his girl and together they went to the middle of the floor. Bill tapped Eduardo on the shoulder and they switched partners. Nancy laughed and started showing Bill the steps.

Sandy and Rollin headed for the floor.

"Come on, Kenny." Sarah grabbed my arm.

"No, Sarah. You know I'm no good at—" But I was being dragged onto the floor.

As Nancy predicted, the Elvis stuff didn't go away. Not completely. But there was a lot less of it after that night. She was only at school half-days during spring semester along with a lot of other kids in vocational programs. I saw her on the street the summer after she graduated.

"Hey, Nancy."

"Hey yourself. How you doing, Ken?"

"Good. How about you?"

She swept her black hair back from her cheek. "Look, no sideburns. I spent my first two paychecks on electrolysis."

"Good for you. Where are you working?"

"At the police station. I'm supposedly a secretary, but I do a lot of interpreting. Sometimes I even get called out in the middle of the night."

"Sounds cool."

"Yeah, it's really surprising how many problems go away when people can talk to each other."

"Going to be a police officer someday?"

She grinned. "Maybe. But I think I'll wait a few years. Right now, I might be tempted to beat the crap out of a few kids with a baton."

"I bet I could guess some names. Is Eduardo still around?"

"Nah, he took off for New Mexico with some buddies. He's a nice guy, but it was nothing serious between us." She winked at me. "So I'm available if you want to give me a call." Before I could fumble an excuse, she poked me in the ribs. "I'm just kidding. I know. You and Sarah. But there are more fish in the pond than Eduardo. And more than you too, Ken Bauer."

She gave me a quick hug before striding off down the street. A big, confident girl with not too bad a profile now that I noticed.

THE OGRE OF MENSA

Featuring:
Ken Bauer, *frequent narrator*
Rollin Acres, *familiar sidekick*
Bill Patchet, *defensive end with large brain*

Even the people who didn't see it happen remember the Thursday Bill Patchet tried to rip the water fountain off the wall. I was there. And he would have done it if Mrs. Tutwieller—who probably weighs ninety-five pounds soaking wet—hadn't marched up to him and yelled: "William, you stop that foolishness right now!"

Big Bill glared down at her, his face still contorted with effort and rage, but he stopped.

"Get in here," she snapped, and marched back into her office. Bill picked up his briefcase and followed her. Not meekly—I don't think Bill's had a meek moment in his life—but with that kind of coiled anger that seemed to vibrate around him most days. Traffic resumed in the hall, but quietly, nobody wanting to talk too loudly in the vicinity of Billy Patch.

"What set him off this time?" Rollin asked me.

"I don't have any idea. Maybe he got less than ninety-eight on a test."

"More likely he got a call from home. He gets a couple a week."

"Whenever the old man is drunk."

"Or beating up on Bill's mom."

"She ought to leave that jerk."

Rollin shrugged. "The old man makes good money. Maybe she thinks the bucks are worth the lumps."

"Yeah, right," I said.

"Just a thought. Must be some reason."

"No good ones."

*   *   *

I doubt that anyone in town likes Bill's dad. Charlie Patchet is this big fat guy with a bad temper, a bad mouth, and a heavy equipment company that he inherited from his daddy. The company pretty much runs itself, and most days Charlie P. is in some bar getting plastered. At 3:00 P.M. he lumbers over to the high school to watch practice for whatever sport Bill's playing that season. During football practice, he used to yell at Bill on every play, but he's been quiet since Coach Carlson threatened to ban him. Of course, that means he just stores up everything until he can really unload on Bill. He always wants Bill to play tougher or smarter or meaner. That's all a load of crap, of course. Bill is already the toughest, smartest, and meanest player on the team. He's a shoo-in for all-conference, possibly all-state, and has a good shot at a division one scholarship for college. But Charlie P. never thinks he plays hard enough.

Bill wasn't at practice that afternoon and neither was his dad. "Do you know what's up?" I asked Rollin.

"Word has it the old man started slapping the old lady around. She called the police this time. Then she called Bill."

"Wouldn't be the first time the cops hauled Charlie P. off."

"Nope. Too bad she always takes him back."

"How the heck can Bill get such good grades with all that going on at home? I wouldn't care about my grades at all."

"You barely care about them now."

"Come on. I do well enough. Just as good as you."

"Yeah, but I barely care about mine."

"Hmm . . . I see what you mean. I guess we shouldn't be expecting any invitations from Mensa, huh?"

"Say what?"

"Mensa. It's the society of the supersmart. Sarah told me about it. You've got to have an IQ of about a gazillion to get in."

"Well, she'd qualify. Bill, too, unless they've got rules against really dangerous smart guys."

"He is a bit of an ogre," I said.

Rollin laughed. "Billy Patch, the Ogre of Mensa. I like that."

"I wouldn't say it to his face."

"Ooohhh, no. Real bad idea."

Sarah picked me up after practice, since the Hammer was getting an overhaul by the shop kids. "Hear about Bill trying to rip the water fountain off the wall?" I asked.

She snorted. "Who hasn't? It'll probably be on the national news."

"Rumor has it that Charlie P. was knocking around Bill's mom again. She called the police and then Bill."

"Figures. Charlie Patchet is one big, fat jerk."

"You're smart. Tell me how Bill can be such a good student with all that crap going on at home?"

"PRS," she said.

"I thought only girls got that."

"PRS not PMS, stupid. It's something I made up to help me study for the psych test on addiction. In the typical addicted family, the oldest kid tries to be perfect, the second is rebellious, and the third is silent. PRS, get it?"

Sarah's going to major in psychology in college, and I love giving her a hard time when she starts getting all intellectual on me. "But how about if there are more than three kids? Does number four turn out to be gay? And maybe number five becomes a serial arsonist. And number six—"

"Stop trying to be difficult. It's just a pattern. Probabilities."

"Just asking. Well, Bill's got a little brother—you know, the kid with the cane—and he's been in some trouble. So I guess he'd fit. I don't know if Bill's even got a sister."

"He does. She's real quiet. So, there you go. PRS."

"I guess. . . . Hey, Rollin and I made up a nickname for Bill today: The Ogre of Mensa."

She laughed. "I like that. Fits Bill to a tee."

We lost 22-21 on Friday when Medford ran in a two-point conversion with a minute remaining. It was a tough loss, and Bill spent an extra minute or two beating the crap out of his locker before heading for the showers. That's when his dad stormed in. "Where the hell were you on that two-point conversion?" he shouted at Bill.

Bill turned slowly and stared down at him.

Confronted with 240 pounds of muscle, sweat, dirt, bruises, and anger, most sensible people would run. Not Charlie P. Instead he started poking Bill in the chest with his forefinger. "If you'd gotten your fat butt down the line, you could have made that tackle! But, no, you were too damned lazy! Big Bill Patchet, hero of the team, gonna be a big-time college ballplayer. Well, let me tell you something. Nobody gets nothing in this world when they quit. When I played, the coach would've had me out behind the stands whaling on me with a piece of two-by-four. But you, you think—"

"Mr. Patchet, that's enough!" Coach Carlson pushed through the crowd to them. "Now you get out of here or, so help me, I'll call the police."

Charlie P. whirled on him. "And you! My twelve-year-old daughter could call a better game than you. If I had your job, I'd—"

Two of the line coaches were there by then, and the three of them started pushing Charlie P. toward the door. They didn't use their hands, just their bulk. I think everyone in the locker room hoped Charlie P. would take a shot at one of them. But he just went on yelling about what a bunch of wimps we all were, coaches included, and his son especially. When the door slammed behind him, nobody said anything. Coach Carlson came back. "Okay, get showered and changed, boys. Bill, come into my office."

"I gotta shower," Bill said, and turned his broad back on all of us.

I showered a couple of places down from Bill. He stood for a long time under the steaming water. Twice I saw him brush at his cheeks, as if wiping away tears, but maybe he just had soap in his eyes.

*   *   *

Monday and Tuesday, Charlie P. was in the bleachers, silent but apparently unashamed about what had happened after the game on Friday. Bill practiced grimly, saying nothing, not even to me, his favorite blocking dummy. I wish I could have said something to him, something sympathetic, but I didn't have the least idea what that might be.

I had chemistry with him on Wednesday. Halfway through class, he was called down to the office to take a phone call. I listened to see if he'd attack a water fountain on his way but heard only his retreating footsteps, sounding slow and discouraged.

He was late for the scrimmage that afternoon, and I was starting to think I'd have an easy practice when Rollin said, "Here's your buddy."

I turned to see Bill striding toward the field, head down, his scraped and battered helmet hanging from his hand. "Crap," I said. "I thought I was going to have an easy day."

Halfway up the bleachers, Charlie P. had taken a seat. He glared down on us, the butt of an unlit cigar clamped in his teeth.

I sighed. "Well, I guess I'd better get ready to take my lumps." Coach Carlson blew his whistle and the offense huddled up around him.

It's not often that I get the better of Billy Patch. But twice that afternoon I managed to get enough of a block on him to let Rollin lead the tailback through the hole to my left. I hesitated. "You okay, Bill? That's twice."

"I know how to count," he growled.

"Sure, Bill. I just wondered if something was bothering you. You know, a knee or your back—"

"Just shut up and play ball."

I shrugged and jogged to the huddle. Coach Carlson stepped in. "Okay, pass play, split end fly, tight end release into the flat."

The Catman frowned. "That's a turkey, Coach. Bill's gonna kill me before I can go long to the split, and he'll knock down anything I throw to the tight in the flat."

"I'm betting he won't get his hands up. He's pretty frustrated right now, and he'll come in low. Just dump it over his head to Bauer. Rollin, you get a piece of him if he gets too far in."

The Catman looked skeptical—we all did—but Carlson was the coach. We lined up. Catman got over the center and yelled: "Down! Set! Thirty-two, twenty-six, hut, hut, *hut*—"

I pushed off, ducking left around Bill, and then cutting hard into the flat, looking back for the pass. Catman was back, waiting for me to clear. Bill came roaring in from the right, intent on nailing him—no-contact jersey be hanged—and Rollin hit him hard just above the right knee. Nothing dirty, nothing out of the ordinary, just a good, hard block. But Bill's spikes caught in the grass, and his knee snapped inward, tearing ligaments, tendons, cartilage, and God knows what all. Catman shifted his feet and threw long for the split end, which was very good thinking, but not what concerned me at that moment.

Rollin and I got to Bill first. He was rolling around, sobbing in short, hard gasps. "Oh, God, Bill. I'm sorry!" Rollin started crying.

"Just hold on, Bill, hold on. Help's on the way," I told him.

Bill grabbed my arm, squeezed tight, and then he started laughing. It was weird. He was laughing, crying, and gasping with pain all at the same time, and for a second I thought he was hysterical. But then he choked out, "Oh, God, I'm happy. I've waited forever for this."

"Bill—" I started.

"I hate this game. I've always hated this damned game. Now it's over."

"Maybe it's not so bad. Maybe just a sprain," I said.

"Na, I felt everything go. It is *over*, man."

Coaches, trainers, and a crowd of the players were there by then. We got Bill to his feet. Rollin got a shoulder under one of Bill's arms, I got a shoulder under the other, and we started for the sidelines, Bill hopping on one leg, still half laughing and half sobbing. Charlie P. charged through the players on the sidelines and out onto the field. "Walk it off, you wimp! Walk it off and get back in the game!" He blocked our way.

"Mr. Patchet," I said. "Bill's hurt and he's hurt bad. His knee—"

He ignored me and stepped close to Bill, his breath reeking of booze. "You get back in the game, boy. Get back in the game, or you're no son of—"

That was when Rollin delivered his second big hit of the day, an open-palm stiff-arm straight to the sternum.

Charlie P. sat down hard on his fat butt. And we left him there, the three of us hobbling toward the sidelines.

Billy Patch never played football again. Within a couple of days, word got around that Mrs. Patchet had kicked the old man out for good. About time, everybody thought.

Bill sat on the sidelines during the last few games of the season, cheering us on and flirting with the girls in the stands while Ramdas clucked around him like some subcontinental mother hen. In school, Bill swung down the halls on his crutches, greeting people who were surprised that he even knew their names.

His knee was still in a cast when basketball season started. After Christmas vacation, Bill started rehabbing down in the weight room. By the time baseball season came around, his knee was about as healed up as it was going to get. But Bill wasn't at the first practice.

Rollin and I saw him in the hall the next morning, still limping a little bit but looking happier than I'd ever seen him. "Hey, Bill," I said, "why weren't you at practice last night?"

He grinned. "I'm not going out. Don't have the time. I've got one of the leads in the spring play."

"The *play?*"

He dropped his voice an octave. "I vill appear as Count Dra-cu-la, despoiler of beautiful young vemen." He winked at us.

We watched him go down the hall, happy as the world's biggest lark. "Billy Patch, the Ogre of Mensa," Rollin mused.

"Dracula of Mensa," I said.

Rollin shook his head. "Doesn't have the same ring to it. I'm sticking with *ogre*. Besides, that accent of his is terrible."

"Bet you five he gets it right by the time the play opens."

"No bet," Rollin said. "I'd never bet against Billy Patch. Not in anything."

THE GULLY

Featuring:

Harry Patchet, *career little brother, part-time criminal*

Bill Patchet, *former defensive end and villain*

Josh Meyer and his father, *plain folk*

Sally, *a horse*

Bill's always looked out for me. And I'm grateful, even if I haven't made it exactly easy for him. So when he got hurt near the end of football season, I was downright gleeful about the chance to look out for him. Don't get me wrong: I wish he hadn't torn up his knee. But I was kind of sick of being the helpless little brother with the crippled leg.

Bill had an ROTC interview in Eau Claire in the week between Christmas and New Year's. We were both off from school, so I graciously volunteered to drive him over. I mean, what were seventy miles of winter roads for an ace driver like me?

The drive over went fine. I sat in a coffee shop, reading the sports section of the paper, while Bill had his interview. We hit a couple of stores and then headed back for Argyle, trying to outrun a big storm coming in from Minnesota. I'd had a good look at the map and figured we could cut off a few miles by taking some county roads. Besides, it would be kind of an adventure.

Right.

We were coming along a straight stretch with a wide, snowy field on the right and deep gully on the left. I'd just leaned over to fiddle with the radio when the deer flashed in front of the car. I slammed on the brakes, just missing the deer but sending the car into a skid. We hit the snow bank on the left side of the road, the front end bucking up so that for an instant sky filled the windshield. Then we were snowplowing down the side of the gully toward death, destruction, and . . . well, what was actually a surprisingly soft landing in a five-foot snowdrift.

"Are you okay?" Bill and I said simultaneously.

"I'm fine," I said. "How about you?"

Bill shifted the cast on his right leg. "I think so. Where'd that stupid deer come from?"

"Out of the ditch on the right. If I hadn't hit the brakes so hard, maybe we—"

He slapped the crippled leg I've lugged around since birth. "Relax, little brother. You did fine. Not your fault we hit a patch of ice."

"I guess," I said, and stared up the track we'd plowed to the bottom of the gully. "Well, no one's going to see us from the road. What do we do now?"

"Call for help, I guess." Bill flipped open his cell phone. After a long minute he sighed. "No service. Not even a twitch."

"Maybe if I blow the horn somebody'll hear us."

"I don't think we passed a house in a couple of miles, but you might as well try."

I leaned on the horn. Nothing happened. "No juice," I said. "Battery must have gotten knocked out of whack. Now what?"

"I haven't a clue," he said.

I stared at him in disbelief. My big brother, the football hero, straight-A student, and all-purpose superstar, didn't have a clue? "*Nada*," he said. "It was ten below when we left, and it'll be twenty below by morning. We are in some serious donkey offal here."

I took a very deep breath. "Then I guess I'd better see if I can climb up to the road."

Bill nodded. "If it weren't for—"

"If it weren't for your cast, you would have been driving and we probably wouldn't be here."

"Will you stop? Not everything is your fault."

I ignored that because it *was,* and I knew it. I rolled down the window and started to lever myself out. "Come on, give me a push."

He did, and I flopped into the snow that buried the car nearly to the windows. Bill handed me my cane and his cell phone. "Take care, huh?"

"Sure. Back in a little while."

A little while. *Right.* I tried edging up the slope sideways, my good leg taking the weight, but I only made it a dozen steps before I slipped and toppled backward. I slid downhill until my coat scooped enough snow down my collar to give me some brakes. Bill rolled down the window. "Come back, Harry. We'll think of something else."

"Like what?" I shouted, and started crawling up the slope.

Cold? There's no word to describe how cold I got. Snow pushed into my sleeves and down the front of my coat. My hands, feet, and kneecaps went numb. Halfway up, I fumbled my cane and watched helplessly as it slid to the bottom of the gully like an errant ski pole. If it had been physically possible, I would have kicked myself. I mean, just how difficult did I have to make this?

I might have quit if I hadn't been so blasted mad at myself. Bill was going to freeze to death if his stupid, incompetent, arrogant, crippled wimp of a brother didn't manage to get to the top of this lousy gully and somehow find help!

Being Bill Patchet's little brother is about my sole identity for most people. Of course, I'm also the second son of Charlie Patchet, prominent drunk and about the meanest guy in Argyle. But I'd rather not own up to that, since being Bill's little brother comes with its own set of problems. Don't get me wrong: Bill's my hero. But that doesn't make me any less jealous of his brains, athletic ability, and the fact he can have any girl he wants to. Life didn't cut me in on any of that. And that pisses me off.

Back a couple of years ago, I decided to even up the score a little. I was in Sound Wave without the money for the CD I wanted. But people don't like to look at crippled people—or whatever the politically correct phrase is this week—and that goes for store clerks, too. So I just slipped the CD into my pocket and stumped out on my cane. I enjoyed the hell out of that. Hey, I deserved a break.

After that I started lifting all sorts of stuff. It's amazing how easy it was. The first couple of times I got caught, I managed to get out of it with my poor, pathetic, little crippled boy act. Then I got busted by a mall cop who didn't buy any of that crap. About the only break I got from him was having my hands cuffed in front of me so I could still use my cane. Dad came down to the police station to get me out and then whipped me good when we got home. And you know what I was thinking? Go to it, old man. I'll just go back for more stuff. And I did.

It wasn't until the third time I got busted that I

started having second thoughts. The judge assigned me to a social worker, and he stuck me in group therapy with a bunch of juvenile offenders. A dozen sessions with those losers and burnouts gave me a new perspective. Not entirely, but I didn't want to join that crowd permanently. So I've laid low for the past year, trying to make up my mind whether I want to go straight or learn how to manage some really worthwhile crime. It's not an easy choice.

My anger got me to the top of the gully. That's when I met the wind coming out of the west and got a whole new education in the meaning of *cold*. I huddled down and managed to get Bill's cell phone open with my numb fingers. Still no service. I was going to have to find a house.

I leaned into the wind, wobbling down the road on my bum leg, my hips wrenching wildly as I fought to keep my balance without my cane. I fell, skinning my palms, got up, stumbled on, and fell again. After that, I kind of lost track. I'd go a ways, fall, get up, stumble a few yards, and fall again. When I fell the last time, the road came up to meet me hard and cold but somehow welcoming, and I just lay there, waiting for everything to be over.

In my dream, I heard the jingle of a harness and the clop of hooves. I lifted my head to see a buggy emerge from the snow blowing across the road. Weird dream, I thought, and let my head fall back to the pavement, which had somehow become soft and warm. But then some survival instinct zapped through my brain. Get your butt off the pavement, stupid! That's an Amish buggy. You might just get rescued here.

I stumbled to my feet and tried to wave with arms that didn't work so well anymore. And just when I didn't think anybody'd ever see me, a deep voice said, "Whoa, Sally."

I could just make out a heavy, bearded face in the shadow of the buggy's interior. It didn't smile. Then a smaller, grinning face popped into view, and a boy about my age hopped down. "Hey," he said, "you got some trouble, huh?"

My voice shook with the cold. "We skidded off the road. My brother's still in the car. He's got this cast on his leg, and by now he's getting real cold and—" I choked back a sob.

"Hey, it's okay," he said. "Come on, we'll go get him." I tried to take a step but fell against him. He caught me. "Are you hurt?"

"No, I was born screwed up."

"Lean on me. I'm Josh Meyer. This is my pa. He understands English fine. Just doesn't like to speak it much."

Mr. Meyer spoke sharply in German. Josh laughed. "Pa says I should stop gabbing and look to the work. He says that a lot where I'm concerned."

Mr. Meyer reached down, lifting me into the seat like I weighed nothing. He peered into my face. "Vere is your *Bruder?*"

"Down in a gully," I said.

"How far?"

"I don't know," I said, and started crying.

"Hey, don't worry," Josh said. "We'll find him." He pulled a blanket across my lap.

Mr. Meyer slapped the reins. "Gid'up, Sally."

Even jammed between Josh and Mr. Meyer, I couldn't quite believe that I was riding in an Amish buggy. A thousand times on the roads of rural Wisconsin I'd passed the farms of the "plain folk," who had chosen to live their Christianity without the conveniences of modern life. I'd seen the men plowing fields behind big workhorses and watched the women hanging simple cotton dresses and denim overalls on clotheslines in the yards. And a few times, when we'd passed their farmhouses at night and seen the glimmer of kerosene lamps in the windows, I'd wondered what it would be like to live their way. But I hadn't wondered much. The Amish were just part of the landscape and of little interest to a town kid like me.

I peered at the snowbanks along the road. Had I made it this far? No, it wasn't possible. We'd missed him. We'd have to turn arou— "There!" I shouted.

Mr. Meyer pulled up, handed Josh the reins, and climbed down. He stood for a minute at the lip of the gully, and then spoke half a dozen sentences in German. Josh said, "We're going to have to pull him up in a blanket. So, sorry, partner, but I'm going to need this." He pulled the heavy blanket from my lap and looped the reins over the seat. "Relax. Sally won't go anywhere."

I couldn't stand not knowing if Bill was all right, so I

climbed down and stood beside the buggy, clinging to one of the wheels for support. The mare turned her head to gaze at me. "It's okay," I said. "I'm, uh, just going to hang on here." She tossed her head and ignored me.

Josh and Mr. Meyer wallowed down through the snow to the car. Mr. Meyer rapped on the frosted window. Nothing happened. He hammered on the roof, waited, and did it again. Oh, God, I thought. Then the window rolled down and a sleepy voice said, "Hey, Harry, that you?"

"I'm up here," I shouted. "Stay awake and help these guys get you out."

Bill is big to start with, and his cast made him a lot bigger in the wrong places, but they managed to get him through the window. They wrapped him in the blanket and started crawling up the slope, pulling him between them. For every two feet they gained, they slid back one, but they made it halfway up before the blanket started slipping out from under Bill. Mr. Meyer grabbed for Bill, and Josh grabbed for Mr. Meyer, and then they were all tumbling down the slope. I think I cried out, because Sally shied and then turned to stare accusingly at me.

I watched helplessly as Josh and Mr. Meyer stumbled over to Bill. Mr. Meyer knelt by him. After a moment, Josh turned and waved to me. "He's okay. Hold on."

They talked for a minute, and then Josh cupped his hands around his mouth. "There's a rope in the back of the buggy. Can you tie one end to the rear axle and throw the other end down here?"

I hesitated. "I guess so."

"Okay. We'll get him up part way."

I found the rope, crawled under the buggy, and tied it to the axle. Then I crawled to the lip of the gully and managed to stand. Josh and Mr. Meyer had gotten Bill just about to where they'd taken the tumble earlier. "Okay, throw it!" Josh yelled.

I heaved the rope and watched as it uncoiled in the air, the end falling just within Josh's reach. First try. Unbelievable. Mr. Meyer bunched the end of the blanket and knotted the rope around it. "Good," Josh yelled. "Now climb up and give Sally a little slap with the reins. Just a touch. She'll understand. Ease her left and let her do the rest."

Not a problem. Uh-huh. I climbed onto the seat, took the reins, mustered my most confident voice, and said, "Go horse. Uh, real slow, okay?" I shook the reins, and she stepped off. I pulled on the left one and she followed. Then I eased up, and she went straight.

"Okay," Josh yelled. "We're up."

Already? We were just getting into this. "Whoa, Sally," I said. She stopped. Amazing.

It was like a time warp. Mr. Meyer lit a lamp in a room straight out of the 1800s: no TV, no carpeting, no radio, not a single electric light. Yet, there was something comforting about the plain furniture and the way everything seemed to be exactly what it was meant to be without any noise or commotion.

Josh bustled around Bill and me, getting our feet out of our frozen shoes and wrapping us in quilts. "Ma and the kids went to visit my aunt for a few days. Pa and I were on the way over to see them when we found you."

"I'm sorry," I said. "We didn't—"

"Hey, don't worry about it."

Mr. Meyer spoke in German from where he was rebuilding the fire in the cast-iron stove. Josh grinned. "Pa says God put us right where He wanted us. You hungry?"

"Sure," we both said.

When they went to the kitchen, Bill reached over and squeezed my arm. "Thanks, little brother. Much longer and I'm not sure I would have come around."

"You're welcome. But I'm sorry—"

"Stop." He leaned over and gave me a hug. "You are something tough, bro. Just too tough on yourself."

Bill's cell phone had found service and still had enough juice for one more call. I called Mom to let her know we were sitting out the storm with a couple of friends. Tomorrow we could give her the whole story.

Josh and Mr. Meyer fed us big bowls of stew and the best bread and peanut butter I'd ever eaten. While Mr. Meyer cleaned up, Josh got us settled in a room with twin beds. "Good night, now," he said, and turned down the kerosene lamp until it barely flickered.

Bill was snoring in two minutes, but tired as I was, I couldn't fall asleep. My leg and my hips ached from all the unaccustomed use. Worse, I couldn't stop blaming myself for everything that had happened. Finally, when the house was quiet, I got up.

I was sitting in a rocker by the stove when I looked up

to see Mr. Meyer in his nightshirt and bathrobe. He hesitated, and then sat down across from me. "You are troubled by something, perhaps?"

I stared down at my bum leg and shrugged. "It's just that I can never quite count on myself. I'm doing okay, and then something like this happens. Then it's kind of hard to trust myself."

He waited until he was sure I was done. "I think you are trustworthy. You saved your *Bruder*."

"Yes, but I put us down in that gully to start with."

"You told us of the deer and the ice and the skid. It was your machine that was unreliable. That is the way with all machines. But you? You did what you needed to do."

I looked at him then, saw him smiling and saw the peace deep in his eyes. "Uh, thanks," I said. "I've never quite looked at things that way before."

His smile widened a little. "You are welcome, though I only tell what I see: a good lad who'll be a good man but now needs a night's rest."

The next morning, Josh took me into town in the buggy to find a tow truck. "Heard you and Pa talking last night," Josh said. "Did he give you his speech about machines?"

"Some of it, I guess." I hesitated. "How do you feel about living this way?"

A new Ford pickup whooshed by us. Josh smiled. "Oh, sometimes I think it'd be fun to try some of the new ways. But most of the time I enjoy how we live. It'd take some explaining, but I don't envy all the temptations you guys live with."

I thought about that. Temptations. Yeah, there were a few around. "Would it surprise you if I told you I'd been busted a few times for shoplifting?"

He pursed his lips. "Not really, I guess. I've felt like doing that. We go into town to Menard's or Fleet Farm, and I see lots of stuff I'd like to have. Just because we live this way doesn't mean we don't want things. You know, like candy, pop, that sort of stuff. We don't get much of that."

"How do you resist?"

He shrugged. "I try to remember what Pa says, that stealing is giving away part of yourself for something you don't really need. Maybe that sounds kind of corny, but I think he's right."

"Yeah, I think he probably is. . . . I like your dad. He kind of scared me at first, but he's a nice guy."

"Yeah, he is. A pain sometimes, but I wouldn't trade him."

"My mom kicked out my old man."

"I'm sorry."

"That's okay. He deserved it. . . . By the way, I quit stealing a while ago."

"Oh. And just when I was going to ask you to pick up some stuff for me." He laughed. "Just kidding."

We rode in silence for a few minutes. Sally trotted along, her breath puffing back to freeze on her coat in white patches. "I guess I ought to pay you and your dad something," I said.

"Nah, Pa'd never take anything. When we get to town, you can buy me an ice-cream cone. And I'll buy you one. That way we'll be straight."

I stared at him in horror. "Not ice cream," I said. "Hot chocolate. Hot, hot chocolate. But not ice cream. Not until next summer."

He grinned. "Okay. Means you'll have to come back to visit."

"You know," I said, "that would be really cool. Hey, do you mind if I drive for a while?"

"Be my guest. Sally won't mind. Just remember, easy does it."

"Yeah," I said. "Easy does it."

STORIES FROM SENIOR YEAR

KICKER WANTED

Featuring:
Ken Bauer, *tight end and holder*
Rebecca "Becks" Campbell, *rugby player*
Matt Sommermeyer, *kicker*
The usual crew

A unt Genevieve split the seam between two business-men and came sprinting down the ramp into Mom's arms. They jumped around like a couple of pom-pom girls celebrating a big win. I spotted my cousin Rebecca trailing behind in the crowd of grouchy folks deplaning from the long flight. "Hey, Becks. Welcome to America."

She squinted at me. "Kenneth?"

"Yep."

"You've grown big."

"Well, it's been five years." I handed her a balloon.

She stared up at it speculatively. "Thank you."

"Sure. You've grown up, too."

She made a face. "I haven't grown a centimeter since I was twelve, except across the bust and bum."

"Uh, yeah," I said. She had a good deal of both, but she didn't look flabby. In fact, she looked solid as all get out.

Mom and Aunt Gen stopped jumping and got weepy. "Oh, terrific," Becks said. "The sisters can't even wait a decent interval before comparing blokes. My dad or your dad, who's the bigger bounder?"

"Well, mine's ancient history," I said. "Let's go get the baggage. Mom's going to bring the car around." We started down the corridor. Becks picked out a little kid and gave him the balloon.

"That was nice," I said.

"Sorry. I suppose I'm a bit old for balloons."

"No, I meant it. That was nice."

"You Americans don't inflect enough. Sometimes it's hard to tell what you mean."

"Oh . . . ," I said. "Hey, I like the way English people talk. No one around here calls people blokes and bounders."

"Something I'll need to change, I suppose."

I rented a couple of carts and we waited for the baggage carousel to start moving. I thought of asking her about Uncle Frank, who'd married Aunt Gen and swept her off to Jolly Old England lo' these many years ago. Instead, I asked her about her older brother, Keith.

"He's fine. He's studying for his A-levels."

"Come again?"

"His college entrance exams. He'll knock 'em cold. He's the family genius."

"You do okay, don't you?"

She shrugged. "I do all right."

The conversation stalled, and before I could think better of it, I heard myself ask: "So, how's Uncle Frank?"

She snorted. "Preening like a jay in May. Got his new bird all set up in a flat in Kensington. He invited me to lunch and brought her along. I suppose so I'd learn to like her."

"And?"

"She's all right for a home wrecker. About twenty with bunches of blonde hair, about six active brain cells, and huge knockers. Amazing, really. The father is quite mesmerized."

Before I could think of anything intelligent or sensitive

to say, she brushed angrily at her eyes and marched off toward the restrooms. Bauer, you're a jackass, I thought. Why'd you go and bring him up?

She came back, face washed and hair combed. The carousel started moving. "I see some of ours," she said, pushing into the crowd and starting to heave the heavy bags to me with angry strength. Yeah, she was solid all right. Solid and strong.

I drove the thirty miles to Argyle while Mom and Aunt Gen talked in the back and Becks dozed in the passenger seat. I rolled down the window and let the late summer night keep me awake. At home, Mom fed us a snack and hustled them off to bed. I called Sarah.

"Hi," she said. "Get the travelers on the ground?"

"Yep. On the ground, home, and to bed. Coming to the scrimmage in Black River tomorrow?"

"Can't. Mom says we have to go to Eau Claire to see my grandma for the weekend. We'll be back Monday night."

"I'd rather you stayed here. You could help me entertain Becks."

"Sorry, duty calls. You can introduce us on Tuesday."

"Fired up for starting school?"

"Sort of, I guess. Not the work but seeing people."

The Black River scrimmage marked the climax of our preseason. We looked better than I thought we would. Catman was sharp at quarterback. Matt Sommermeyer drilled a forty-yard field goal from my hold—an almost unheard of distance for high school. Rollin blasted some good holes from his fullback spot. And yours truly looked not too bad at tight end with four catches and a nearly perfect day blocking.

My punting was more of an adventure. I was new to the job and the coaches had kept hard rushes off me in practice. But the Black River kids were all competing for jobs and wanted a piece of the ball or a piece of me. Twice our line gave me time to get off decent kicks, but the protection broke the third time and I obliged by shanking the ball into the crowd. Mom had a chance for a nice catch but ducked. Becks caught the ball on the first bounce, examined it with a frown, and then casually pooch-kicked it to the ball boy.

Back on the sidelines, Catman grinned at me. "Better not shank another one, Bauer, or that beefy babe might take your job."

"Watch it, shrimp. That normal-sized person is my cousin."

He snickered. "Big butts run in the family, huh?"

Rollin growled, "Play football, guys."

I let it go; Catman is never worth the trouble.

Becks registered for school on Monday, a teacher workday before school began. I helped her find her classrooms and introduced her to her teachers. Mr. Larkin, her chemistry teacher, raised his eyebrows. "England, huh? I coach girls' soccer. We could use some help if you're a player."

Up to this point Becks had been pretty passive about the introductions: polite but not real interested. Now her lip curled in disgust. "I play rugby."

He laughed. "Rugby? A couple of my frat brothers played rugby. I thought girls had better sense."

Becks gave him a frozen look of death.

"So," I chirped, "we'll see you later, Mr. Larkin."

"Sure. Let me know if you change your mind about soccer, Rebecca."

Out of earshot, she growled: "Twit. It'll be a cold day in Hades when I play soccer." She glanced at me. "Know anything about rugby?"

"Not really. I've flipped by a couple of games on cable. It, uh, didn't really impress me."

She snorted. "You should have watched longer. I'd like to see your fat football players try to run with our team. What's your pitch? A hundred meters?"

"Pitch?"

"Field."

"A hundred yards by a hundred and sixty feet."

She snorted. (Boy, she did that a lot.) *Yards and feet.* I forgot you Americans are still in the Dark Ages. New World, my bum."

She'd been zinging the ol' U. S. of A. pretty regularly, and this time I got defensive. "Well, you still use *stone* for body weight, don't you?"

"Not the same at all. That's tradition. Something you colonists might have someday."

I introduced her to Mrs. Sparks, her language arts

teacher, and waited in the hall while they talked. Patience, I told myself. Before long she'll have her own friends.

Seconds after dismissing Mrs. Sparks as "utterly past it," Becks was back on rugby. "So, your football pitch is ninety-one meters long and forty-nine wide, huh?"

"Something like."

"A rugby pitch is a hundred meters long by seventy wide. Shall we work out the square meters?"

"No, I get your point. Might as well tell me the rest."

With relish, she did. "We play fifteen on a side, two forty minute periods, no protective equipment, no substitutions."

"So you must not tackle."

"Oh, we tackle. That's the best bit."

I'll bet, I thought. "So how do you score?"

"You can run the ball in for five or kick it through the goalposts for three. There's also a two-point conversion kick and a three-point penalty kick. I like kicking, too." We paused at the door of her math classroom. "Please don't make this teacher a twit," she muttered. She squared her shoulders and marched in, me trailing.

I didn't have any classes with Becks, so I didn't see her in action that first week. Sarah did. At lunch in the cafeteria on Thursday, she said, "Your cousin isn't making a big hit with the girls."

"What's happened?"

"Nothing real big. She's just standoffish and real quick to snap at people."

"She's like that around the house. I think she's home-sick."

"That's not our fault."

Sandy Dunes plopped down next to us. "Did you hear what your cousin said in English class?"

"No, but I've got a feeling you're about to tell me."

"You bet I am. Sparks has us reading this poem 'Kubla Khan.' And Becks tells this story about how the poet Coleridge said he fell asleep one afternoon and dreamed the whole thing but didn't get the ending because somebody came and 'knocked him up.'"

I almost choked on a bite of macaroni. "You're kidding!"

She grinned. "Not a bit. And, boy, did people howl. Matt Sommermeyer had to leave the room. Said he was going to pee his pants if he didn't get to the bathroom. Mrs. Sparks was real nice, explaining that Becks meant someone knocked on Coleridge's door and woke him up, not that someone came and made him pregnant. But Becks got real red and left in a big huff when the bell rang."

I sighed. "She should have laughed it off."

"Yep, she should have. People *are* trying to be nice to her. Kendra asked her if she was going to try out for basketball or gymnastics. But Becks said she only played rugby. And you know what that jerk Marvin Katt said? 'Hey, maybe you ought to go out for wrestling. You got some beef.' I thought she was going to brain him."

"Tempting solution to some problems," Sarah said.

"Tempting," I said. "But who plays quarterback if we don't have the Catman?"

Football players don't get many days off, and we practiced that afternoon in a steady rain. When the special teams split off to run drills, I lugged a bag of balls to the far end of the field. Matt was limbering up his leg, about the only player without a coat of mud and slime. I handed the bag to Rollin. "Let's keep this short. I'm tired."

"Tell that to Matt. He'll stay out here until dark if we let him."

"Let's go, guys," Matt yelled.

I went back to where Matt had already set his tee and knelt to receive Rollin's snap. "Rollin and I are going to do a couple snaps first. I want to get my fingers so I can feel them again."

"Sure. Don't want you to lose those." Matt bounced on his toes, all grinning impatience, as usual. Rollin snapped the ball and I got it down with passable precision. "Bang! And it's away," Matt yelled, imitating a TV announcer. "It's hooking . . . hooking . . ."

I sighed and signaled for Rollin to send the next one back my way. I shouldn't complain too much. Most teams assign a quarterback to do the holding, but Catman wasn't about to risk his precious pinkies, and Jim Braehm, our backup quarterback, is a tad too jumpy for the job. I enjoy it. Matt was bound to set some records this year, and Rollin and I would be part of that.

We did some extra points and then started working our way back with steadily longer field goals. By the time Matt hit a thirty-five-yarder on his third try, my hands were sore and I was very sick of kneeling in the wet grass.

"Enough," Rollin called. "I'm tired of looking at you two through my legs."

"And we're tired of looking at your butt," I said. "What d'ya say, Matt?"

"I want to try one from forty."

"Ha," I said. "That'll be the day."

"Hit from forty at Black River."

"That was with a big tail wind."

"No way. There was barely a breeze."

"Let's get it over with," Rollin called.

Matt reset his tee, I knelt, and Rollin snapped the ball to me. I caught it smoothly, dropped the nose on the tee, and spun the laces so they faced the end zone. In the next split second Matt's right foot was supposed to hit the ball, leaving the space beneath my hand uncannily empty, as if the ball had vaporized. Instead a bomb went off in my left ear as his kicking foot hit my helmet, knocking me face flat in the muddy grass. I rolled over to see Matt writhing in pain, his plant foot twisted awkwardly under him.

You'd think a guy's best buddy might check on him when he goes down with a head injury, but Rollin bypassed me to see to Matt. I stumbled up and went over to help.

Now Matt may be a kicker, but he's also one very tough kid. He managed to sit up. He held out a hand to Rollin. "Help me up, man."

"You sure?" I said.

"Yeah. Come on, before the coaches think something's wrong."

We hauled him up. But the second he tried to put

weight on his plant foot, he staggered. "Here. Hold on to us," Rollin said. "We'll help you walk it off."

But in three steps, we had to lower him to the ground. He stared at his foot, his face gray with pain. "Damn!" he said. "That's my season. I thought it was okay, but it must not have healed all the way since I dumped my four-wheeler." He unsnapped his chinstrap, threw his helmet on the ground, and sat with his face in his hands.

Trainers, assistants, and coaches arrived and we were pushed back to the edge of the crowd. Catman came striding over. "Well, you dopes really messed it up this time! Who's gonna kick now?"

I looked at him with loathing. "Do you really think that's the most important question right now?"

"Go away, Catman," Rollin said.

Catman strode off. "*Kicking!* Another thing I'll have to do."

I could hear Becks yelling when I opened the back door. Mom intercepted me. "Come on. We're going out to eat."

"Huh?"

"You and me. Out to eat."

"What's going on?"

"I'll tell you about it in the car." Once we were underway, she sighed. "Becks came home upset. I guess some kids at school laughed at her. Genevieve tried to make light of it, and Becks just exploded. Blamed her mother for her parents' breakup, the move here, everything. It's been building for a while, whatever set her off."

I grimaced. "Well, she said something pretty funny in English class." I told the story.

"Oh, boy," Mom said. "Well, she'd better get used to American ways. The divorce papers came express mail today."

We ate at the Swedish Buffet, my favorite restaurant in town, the lutefisk excepted. Back home things were quiet: Becks in her room, Aunt Gen weeping on the couch. I grabbed a can of pop and headed for my room.

Friday night we played Montrose in a nonconference game. They were plucky but a lot smaller, and we scored touchdowns pretty much at will. Good thing, since we didn't have anyone who could kick an extra point, much less a field goal. Coach Carlson tried four different guys on extra points, including Catman twice. Five tries, five misses, several harrowing moments for the holder who'd hoped to go through life with a full set of fingers. (Catman blamed his misses on me, of course.) We won 30–7, but it wouldn't be so easy once we started playing conference games.

As usual, a lot of fans came onto the field after the game to shake hands with the players and coaches. Becks took the opportunity to confront Coach Carlson. "I can kick the bloody ball if your blokes can't!"

He stared at her. "I beg your pardon?"

"I can kick the bloody ball. Through the goalposts. To score the points."

I stepped in. "Coach, I guess you haven't met my cousin Rebecca Campbell. She just moved here from England."

"Glad to meet you, young lady."

"I play rugby back home. Our team doesn't have a lot of *ladies,* but we kick balls."

I gazed at the sky for aid. Coach Carlson hid a grin. "I'm sure you do."

"So do I get a try? Or doesn't your American football let girls play?"

"Well, it's unusual."

"But it's not against the rules?"

"No. Auburndale has a girl on the roster as a defensive back. She doesn't play very . . ."

"Then I'll show you this instant. Kenneth, where's that friend of yours? The one with the peculiar name."

"Here I am," Rollin said.

"Monday," Coach Carlson said. "If you can really kick extra points, that'll be time enough to find out."

No way Becks was going to wait until Monday to practice. Saturday, Rollin and I worked with her for two hours. Becks was as good as her word: She could kick the bloody ball. The kicking transformed her. She bounced with excitement before every kick, whooped when they sailed through the uprights, yelled in frustration when she missed. Sarah and Sandy, who were shagging balls for us, got in the spirit, and pretty soon we were all cheering or groaning.

Monday, dressed in shorts, her rugby jersey, and the smallest set of spikes we could find, she won the job. Only Catman and a few other Neanderthals complained about having a girl on the team. Coach Carlson slapped them down. "Rebecca is our teammate. Nothing else matters. You guys block for her, protect her, give her all the help you can." He stared at Catman. "All of you."

Becks rode beside me with the football jersey on her lap. "The colonists are going to let me play football."

"Yep. Looks that way."

"When do I get to tackle somebody?"

"You won't have to. Not on extra points."

She frowned. "How about on those long kicks? You know, at the start of the game and after a score."

"Kickoffs. Sid Halverson has that job. He can kick it a mile, just not very straight."

"I can kick that far."

"I don't know, Becks. Sid's got a big leg. Besides, we need to concentrate on the extra points."

"How about penalty kicks?"

I reminded myself that she'd only seen a scrimmage and one football game. "No penalty kicks in our game. Just kickoffs, punts, extra points, and field goals."

"How about a field goal? Do I get to hit anyone then?"

"Not unless it's blocked and recovered by someone on the other team. And Becks, Coach Carlson said just to concentrate on extra points. Not many high school teams even try field goals. Not unless they've got somebody like Matt, and you haven't even been in a game yet."

She stuck out her lower lip and then grinned. "All right. But don't count on things staying that way."

*　　*　　*

All that week she was an entirely different person. She practiced hard, made up with Aunt Gen, didn't talk about going back to England, didn't zing America or the "colonists," and even made a couple of friends in school. Friday night Sandy and Sarah helped her suit up in the girls' locker room. She came out to warm-ups looking a little awkward in her equipment but pleased as anything. "How you doing?" I asked.

"Terrific. Let's kick some bum."

We did okay, beating Medford 27-10. Becks missed her third extra point, but three for four wasn't bad for a first game. Not that she thought so, and Saturday we practiced another two hours.

Against Rhinelander the next Friday she was a perfect five for five as we ran our record to 3-0 with a 35-14 win. But the following Friday in the rain and mud at Riter's Point, we were pathetic, missing tackles, fumbling, and generally making fools of ourselves. Becks missed three extra points, including the one that would have tied the game 19-19 early in the fourth quarter. But Point went on to score two more touchdowns on turnovers, and even Catman couldn't blame the loss on her. Still, Becks was down in the dumps all weekend.

With Slayton, the defending conference champs, coming up, we practiced our rear ends off all the next week. Becks kicked until I made her stop. "You've got to keep your leg fresh."

"I can do a few more. Come on."

"Nope. Hit the showers."

"About all I get to hit," she muttered.

"Don't grouch. The game's tomorrow. Time for the right attitude."

She stuck her tongue out at me.

Friday night, big game, the air crisp, the stands full. Things don't get a lot better. The first quarter went fast, Slayton using most of it on a long running drive that put them ahead 6–0. When their kicker shanked the extra point, one of our assistant coaches said to another: "It doesn't look like we're the only ones with kicking problems."

Becks gave him her death-ray glare. "Head in the game, Becks," I said.

She snorted. "Why bother? I hardly ever get to do anything."

We got a good return on the kickoff, and I went out to play tight end. We went to the air, Catman throwing on five consecutive downs. I caught one for a first down and spent the rest of the time blocking. With their linebackers dropping into coverage, we started mixing in some runs, scoring three minutes into the second quarter.

Becks jogged out, placed her tee, and measured off her steps. The rest of us set up in position and the play went off just as it should, Becks's kick hooking a little to the left but still safely within the uprights. Argyle 7, Slayton 6.

Neither team did anything notable until we recovered a fumble on their thirty with barely forty seconds to go in the half. Catman threw, missed, threw and hit Rollin for six, threw and missed. Fourth down, ball on the twenty-four with fifteen seconds to go in the half. Coach Carlson called our final time-out and jogged toward the huddle. I gauged the distance for a field goal. Adding ten yards for the end zone, it would be a thirty-four-yard kick. Long, but possible. We were at the middle of the field, the wind calm, our line playing well. Why not?

"Coach—" I said.

"Don't even start. I already told her 'no way.' Now listen up, men. Here's what's going to work."

He called a play that put three receivers in the end zone, but the Slayton coach rolled the dice, calling an all-out blitz that sacked Catman before he could get the ball off. Halftime score: still Argyle 7, Slayton 6.

"I could have made that kick," Becks snapped as we walked down the hall to the locker rooms.

"I know," I said. "But let it go. Coaches don't like distractions at halftime."

"I'm not a distraction!"

Tell that to the coaches, I thought. Ms. Stepping, one of the female gym teachers, intercepted Becks at the door of the boys' locker room. "Come over to the girls', Becks. I'll help you with whatever you need."

"I'm fine. I want to be with the team."

"Nope, we're under orders. This way, young lady."

A couple of the team's Neanderthals hooted. Becks glared at them, her look chipping tile off the wall behind them. "I am not a lady. I play rugby. Remember that, you cretins."

Inside the locker room, Rollin shook his head. "Wow, she had me reaching for my crucifix. How do you protect yourself?"

"Garlic. A whole chain of it around my neck."

"Is that what smells so bad?"

Halftime in a locker room with forty guys who've been playing a contact sport for nearly an hour is not a place for anyone overly sensitive to body odor. Fortunately, the time goes fast. The coaches huddled with their units while guys got various bodily functions out of the way. "All right," Coach Carlson called. "We've got another half of football to play. Everybody concentrate on what we've practiced. Do that and we'll win this ball game. Break 'em down, Rollin."

"Breakdown team!" Rollin shouted, "Reeaaddy, breakdown . . ."

"Team!" We shouted in unison. And believed it.

Becks came up to me while the special teams got the second half started. "Did you talk to him?"

"Becks, it wouldn't have done any good. He's not about to let you try something we haven't practiced."

"You and I kicked a few."

"Just for fun and never in a game. Relax. Concentrate on hitting the extra points."

We pounded the ball downfield with runs and short passes. Twice Catman changed plays at the line because he wanted to throw deep. Coach called time, ripped into him, and we went back to work. Rollin got the score on a straight-ahead blast from three yards out and we were up by seven: Argyle 13, Slayton 6.

Becks came out for the extra point. I glanced at Rollin, who was kneading his left biceps. "You okay?"

"Yeah, I'm okay. Just a little stinger."

Maybe it was the stinger, maybe just a momentary miscalculation, but his snap sailed high. I snared the ball, swung it down fast, nose on the tee, and got my hand clear just as Becks's foot hit leather. No chance. The ball bounced off the back of one of our blockers and dribbled off to the right. One of the Slayton players picked it up and looked around for an official to hand it to. That's when Becks hit him, high up in the chest and hard. The ball flew up in the air, settling like a wounded duck in my arms. "Run!" Becks screamed.

Run? For a second I was almost confused enough to do it. Instead, I tossed the ball underhand to an official. "You can't advance a blocked extra point," I said. "Not after it hits the ground."

She untangled herself from the Slayton player. "But in rugby—"

"This isn't rugby. Remember?"

One of our guys jogged past. "Way to go, girl. You just cost us fifteen yards."

She looked at me. "What?"

I pointed to the yellow flag behind her. "Personal foul. Fifteen-yard penalty." I looked over her shoulder at the Slayton player, who'd struggled up and was checking his body for broken parts. "Sorry about that, man. She's new to the game."

"Don't teach her any more. Man, that was a shot." He headed for his sidelines.

"Come on, Becks," I said.

For some reason a big penalty at change of possession always puts the defense out of whack. Spotted fifteen yards on the kickoff, Slayton hit us for a quick score on a couple of good runs and a long pass. Their kicker made the extra point and we were tied: Argyle 13, Slayton 13.

The defenses dominated the rest of the third quarter and most of the fourth. Becks stood by herself, fuming. I went over to her. "Look, you made a mistake. Now put it behind you and get ready to make the next kick. Just remember it's not a game of rug—"

"I know what bloody game it is!"

"Hey, don't bite my head off. I didn't blindside that guy."

Midway through the fourth quarter I had to punt from our end zone. Joy, o joy. I moved back to the end line, careful not to step out, took the short snap, and tried to get my foot into it. But the ball was barely off my toe when a Slayton rusher laid out in front of me. The ball must have hit him squarely in the stomach because he let out a "Woof!" Then twenty-two guys were scrambling for the ball. I got to it first, doing my own lay out and managing to swat it past the end line before two Slayton linemen landed on top of me. Safety. Two points. Argyle 13, Slayton 15.

We had to give them a free kick, and I punted the ball from our twenty. I got off a good one, and the defense came through to stop them three and out. Still, we only had two and a half minutes left when we fielded Slayton's punt with a fair catch on our own thirty-five. I'll hand it to Catman: He didn't get flustered, moving us steadily downfield against their prevent defense. We got a first down on their seventeen with thirty-three seconds to play. This could still be done. I went on an out pattern that should have given us eight or ten yards, but their strong safety read the play, cut in front of me, and would have made the interception if I hadn't grabbed him by the back of the jersey. Offensive pass interference: fifteen yards and loss of down.

Catman and I traded glares in the huddle. "Play football," Rollin growled.

Starting from the thirty-two, Catman missed the split end on second down and then hit the flanker for thirteen on third down. With seven seconds to go, he called our final time-out. Ball on the nineteen, fourth down, behind by two points. You do the math.

Coach Carlson joined us. "Can she do it, Bauer?"

"Huh?"

"Kick a field goal from here."

"Now wait a second!" Catman snarled.

"Yes, sir. Yes, she can."

Coach pointed at Catman. "Go."

Catman left with the other players not on the field-goal team. Becks set up her tee. "Now just relax," I said. "It's only twenty-nine yards."

"Cousin, hush. And you know all those nasty things you've said about me?"

"What nasty things?"

She winked at me. "Well, I'll forgive them all if you get the ball down for me to kick."

The ball came out of the shadow beneath Rollin. I had it, my fingers finding the laces and spinning it as the nose touched the tee. And she kicked it with plenty of power, plenty of follow-through, and it would have been perfect except this big Slayton lineman managed to get his hand about twelve feet in the air. The ball caromed off his palm and back toward us, tumbling like a shot goose. Becks had it on the fly, sprinted to the right, dropped it, and swung her foot into it as it bounced off the ground. And just as it should have the moment before, the ball sailed through the uprights and into the night.

I've never heard silence fall so fast over so many people. Then pandemonium. Players screamed at each other and started pushing. Officials threw flags and hats and waded in to break things up. The coaches on both sidelines went berserk. I can't even guess what was going on in the stands, but it wasn't pretty.

Becks squatted down, hands over her face. I walked over and put a hand on her shoulder. She looked up at me, tears running down her cheeks. "I forgot. I forgot it wasn't stupid rugby."

"Hold on," I said. "Something's still happening."

The officials held a long conference, finally seeming to agree. The ref stepped clear and raised both arms. The place went nuts.

"What?" Becks screamed. "What?"

"It's good!" I yelled back. "We won!"

She jumped in my arms as our teammates flooded around us, whooping, hugging, and slapping each other on the back. Above us, the public address announcer boomed: "Well, folks. That was a field goal by drop-kick. I've been in this booth for every game for thirty years and I've never seen one before, but dropkicks *are* legal in Wisconsin high school football. So the final score is Argyle sixteen, Slayton fifteen. Congratulations to the young men on both teams for a great game. And to one special young lady."

"I'm not a lady!" Becks growled. Then she grinned. "This is corking fun! Put me down, cousin. I've got some people to thank."

I gave her a final squeeze. "Bloody fantastic, kid. You're a football bloke now." She winced, whether from the squeeze or my assumed accent I couldn't tell.

"Bollocks," she said. "I'm a rugby player."

THE BRIEFCASE

Featuring:
Chad Eilers, *private person*
Randy "the Doughnut" Schmidtke,
  offensive tackle and boogeyman
Veronica "Ronnie" Hainz, *talented*
  impromptu actor
Trish Draves, *femme fatale*
Marvin "the Catman" Katt, *quarterback*
and bimbo target

F ear is not one of my favorite emotions. If my friends want to see a slasher movie, fine; I'll catch the Disney cartoon next door. I figure there's enough stark terror in real life. Witness the September morning I opened a birthday present to discover *the briefcase.*

"You're kidding," I gurgled.

"Isn't it beautiful?" Mom stroked the dark brown leather.

Dad beamed. "Straight from the best leather goods store in Chicago. About time someone at Argyle West showed a little class."

"Dad, no one carries a briefcase to high school! Not mine, anyway."

"Exactly. You'll start a trend. In a few months, we'll raise the tenor of the whole place."

"Tenor?"

"Character, habitual condition. Atmosphere, if you will."

"I'm going to raise the character of Argyle West by starting a briefcase fad? Come on, Dad! The jocks will kill me. That's if I should live so long. My own friends will probably snuff me to avoid humiliation by association."

"Nonsense. The kids who count will adopt the style."

"Why? Everybody's got a backpack."

"Have you ever seen lawyers, businessmen, or judges carrying their papers in a backpack? This will work, Chad. Trust me." He glanced at his watch. "I've got to go. Happy birthday, son. I'll see you at supper." He gave me a slap on the shoulder and Mom a peck on the lips.

"But, Dad . . ." I croaked.

Strangely enough, there's an explanation for all this: My parents are incurable snobs. Me, I'm a democratic, go-with-the-crowd kind of guy. I'm comfortable with jeans, anonymity, and a backpack for my books. Not them. As Mom says: "This family has standards and agendas." Yep, them we got.

On the ride to school, I tried to convince Mom that the local peasantry tends to deal harshly with those who too visibly adhere to elitist standards and agendas. That is, the stuck-up die miserable deaths.

She got downright testy on the issue. "Chad, your father and I have talked about this at length! If I had my way, you'd go to school in Oxfords, decent slacks, and a tie."

"No shirt?"

"Don't be a smart aleck. A briefcase will set the right tone for the fall of your sophomore year. You've had a year to get used to high school, and now it's time for you to make a statement."

"I don't want to make a statement."

"In this world you have to assert who you are. You've been brought up to have standards and agendas. Now is the time to stand by them."

"A briefcase will make me look like a geek."

"It will not. It will make you look . . . professional. That's it, professional."

"Mom! It's a social death warrant."

"Pooh. It's anything but. Now watch for traffic when you get out."

As she roared off, I seriously considered throwing myself under the wheels of the first oncoming car. But they all stopped, and I crossed the street in a crowd of other kids. I was very conscious of stares, whispers, and a certain edging away, as if the briefcase contained radioactive material or some deadly and ill-tempered animal of indeterminate species.

My locker was only a long hallway from the main entrance, and I scuttled the distance without attracting serious abuse. I think most kids were too disconcerted to comment. A kid carrying a briefcase was sort of like seeing a pink ostrich waltzing down the hall: a vision so hallucinogenic that some kids no doubt wondered if they'd contracted brain damage over the weekend.

Melinda Riolo and Don Shadis caught me trying to stuff the briefcase into my locker. "Is that what I think it is?" Don asked.

"Yep," I said. "Big birthday present."

"Wow," Melinda said. "Why didn't they just give you a cobra? Death would have been quicker."

"And a lot less painful," Don said. "Are you nuts, man? You can't carry that thing around here."

I had the briefcase on end and was throwing my weight against the locker door. No luck.

"It's not going to fit," Melinda said.

"She's right," Don said. "Leave it in the hall. Someone will turn it in to the lost and found and you'll be permanently rid of the thing."

"It's got my name inscribed on the inside and my initials on the front."

"Classy," Melinda said.

"Fatal," Don said. "Well, good luck, man. Don't let the Doughnut catch you with that thing."

Whatever dumb shock first greeted the sight of my briefcase evaporated within a couple of hours. I was called nerd, dork, wuss, dweeb, geek, and pencil-neck by the rankly abusive. The more witty offered comments about my needing a tie and a pocket protector. The hands-on critics punched, passed, and kicked the offending item. Still, as Dad had bragged, the briefcase came from the best leather goods store in Chicago and didn't show a scuff. I wasn't holding up nearly so well.

I was on my way to German class between fifth and sixth period when I ran into Rollin Acres and Ken Bauer. I tried to push my way past them, but they sidestepped in unison. "It can't be," Rollin said.

Ken stepped close and peered intently into my eyes. "Bill, is that you in there? Billy Patch, can you hear me?"

"It can't be reincarnation, Ken," Rollin said. "Bill just graduated; he didn't die."

"Yeah, but Ramdas says the spirit—"

"Yeah, sure, whatever." Rollin looked at me. "Seriously, man, are you Bill Patchet's cousin or something?

You're a lot smaller and I don't see any family resemblance, but. . . ."

By this time I was getting pretty sore. "What are you guys blathering about?" I snapped, which wasn't exactly the tone to adopt with two seniors twice my size.

"Bill Patchet," Ken said. "Big defensive end who graduated last year. He was the last kid around here with guts enough to carry a briefcase. Of course, he was six-four and around two-forty. No one messed with Billy Patch."

They actually seemed genuinely curious. "Look," I said. "I got the briefcase for my birthday and my parents are making me carry it."

"Bummer," Rollin said.

"Sounds like child abuse to me," Ken said. "Don't let the Doughnut catch you with it. Could go hard on you."

Their warning was about the eighth I'd received regarding Randy Schmidtke, the football team's huge left tackle. This year's program had him listed at three hundred pounds, approximately six times his IQ. Big boy, dim bulb.

Somehow I made it through the day and slunk home a back way without major incident. But at supper I was completely unable to explain my predicament to Mom and Dad. Maybe that makes me sound like a super wuss, but I don't like to fight and I don't like to hurt people's feelings. Unless it involves committing a felony, I just go along.

My bad temper showed, and Dad came to my room while I was staring morosely at my algebra text. "Your mother's feelings are kind of hurt."

"I'm sorry."

"It's just that she shopped very hard for that brief-case. She studied a lot of catalogs and websites for just the right one. She truly agonized over it, and your in-gratitude hurts her."

"It's not ingratitude, Dad. I appreciate the present, but I just don't want to carry a briefcase to school. No one else does, and I don't want to be singled out."

"Chad, we've always taught you to be true to yourself. Don't follow the crowd, don't give in to peer pressure. Be your own person."

"But, Dad, suppose carrying a briefcase isn't who—"

The phone rang and he turned. "I think this is a call I've been waiting for. Just think about what I said. Don't follow the herd. Sheep never stand out one from an-other."

"I thought sheep traveled in flocks," I said to his back, but I guess that was nit-picking. I wasn't a sheep or a steer, but I was very much afraid of becoming a goat. A sacrificial one.

Mom was her usual upbeat self the next morning when she dropped me at school. And, yes, I had my briefcase in hand. It still wouldn't fit in my locker.

The second day was worse than the first. I was now a personage: the nerd with the briefcase. I learned to walk close to the wall, protecting the briefcase from the casual kick or grab. I heard all the names of the day before plus a new one. I was passing a knot of giggling girls when I first heard *squeegee* applied to a human being. That human being was, of course, me. I pondered the word, wondering what on earth had prompted its association with me. It did have a certain poetic ring, I suppose, since my nerves were now making the sort of pathetic squeaks that a squeegee makes on a dirty window.

By noon, things had turned positively surreal. A teacher I barely knew pulled me into a doorway. He loomed. "Do you know who I am?"

"Uh, Mr. Linquist?"

"Right. I coach special teams. You ever played football?"

"A couple of years in junior high, but as you might notice, I'm not real big."

"Doesn't make any difference. Not if you've got the guts. I need a wedge-breaker, and I think you might be just the guy."

"Wedge-breaker?"

"On kick returns. Someone to break the blocking wedge. Just go down hell-for-leather and throw yourself into the wedge forming in front of the ball carrier. Break it up so other guys can get through to make the tackle. You don't have to be big, but you've got to be fearless. Take on five, six guys at once."

"I . . . I think you've got me confused with somebody else."

"You're the kid with the briefcase, aren't you?"

"Yeah."

"Then you're the guy I want. Any kid with guts enough to carry a briefcase can break a wedge."

I took a breath. "It's not voluntary. I got the briefcase for my birthday. I'd lose it somewhere if I dared."

His face drooped. "Oh . . . You sure of that?"

"I'm afraid so, Coach."

"Maybe you could—"

"I don't think so, Coach. I'm sorry."

He grimaced. "Well, better not let the Doughnut catch you with it. He wouldn't understand."

Immediately after school, I headed downtown to throw myself on Dad's mercy. Somehow this had to stop. So far I hadn't run into the Doughnut, but my luck and nerves wouldn't last forever. Briefly I let my imagination run with fantasies of playing football. If only I did have the guts to break a blocking wedge. Guts and a little more size. But if I admitted the truth, I was a kid more likely to carry a briefcase. Still it was nice to dream.

I took the elevator to the fifth floor of the Fulbright National Bank building. Paula, Dad's secretary, looked up from her desk. "Hi, Chad. Hey, nice briefcase. Is that your dad's?"

"Uh, no. It's mine."

"Oh, really? I didn't think briefcases were in fashion for kids."

"They're not. Is Dad in?"

"Nope. At a meeting across town. I think he'll drop back here before he goes home. Want to leave a message?"

"No, that's okay. I'll see him at home. Wouldn't want to buy a briefcase, would you?"

"No, thanks. The other girls would think I was putting on airs."

"Too bad," I said.

I clumped down the back stairs rather than take the elevator and emerged onto Lexington just in time to run into Marvin Katt, the school's hotshot quarterback, and Trish Draves, widely considered Argyle West's hottest babe. The Catman grinned. "Hey, briefcase boy. How's the life?"

I saw Trish's sculpted ruby lips form simultaneously around a smile and a word. It was at that instant that the first bullet ricocheted off the lamppost two feet behind the Catman's head and two guys in fedoras burst from the doors of the bank. A black '36 Packard roared around the corner and careened toward them. They were shooting wildly, bullets scattering pedestrians and chunks of pavement and brick. The Catman jumped in front of Trish but took two in the chest and one in the abdomen. He sprawled, trying to drag Trish down with him. Desperately, I tried to shield them with my briefcase. A .45 bullet pierced the leather side, plowing to about page 338 of my biology book. More bullets slammed into the briefcase, hammering me back. But I held my position, protecting the girl I'd always loved and the guy I'd always worshipped, offering my life so that they might live on to marry and have children and grandchildren who they would someday tell about "the briefcase boy" who had sacrificed himself for their love.

The bank robbers leaped on the running board of the

Packard, and the driver hit it hard, smoke billowing from screeching tires. A fourth robber burst from the bank, firing a tommy-gun back into the interior. They didn't wait for him. With a curse he threw aside the tommy-gun, pulled an automatic from a shoulder holster, and sprinted our way. "You, blondie!" he shouted at Trish. "Come here!"

No way. I hadn't gone through all this to let him grab Trish as a hostage. I grabbed the handle of the briefcase with both hands and whirled like a hammer-thrower gaining momentum. The briefcase wasn't an aerodynamically impressive missile, but when I let go it had plenty of velocity. It chopped through the air like a loose helicopter blade and caught the guy squarely in the neck. His pistol discharged in the air, the stray bullet neatly skewering a circling seagull. The bad guy staggered back, clutching his shattered windpipe, and collapsed against the wall of the bank as the seagull hit the pavement at his feet with the sickening crunch of tiny bones.

I dropped to one knee beside Trish and the Catman. He was still breathing, but a thin trickle of blood ran from the side of his mouth. Trish was sobbing, clutching him, begging him not to die. He patted her hand. "You'll be all right. It's gonna be okay. I was never right for you. Down deep I'm nothing. Just a jock." He looked at me and tried to grin. "Thanks, buddy. You had it when it counted. Shoulda had you on the team."

"Hold on," I said. "Help's on the way."

"No, no. It's all over for me."

"Oh, Marvin," Trish sobbed. "Don't leave me."

"I gotta, babe. Really gotta go." With a tremendous effort, he managed to lift her hand to place it in mine. "Look after her, buddy," he choked. "You're the guy with the guts and the brains. You're twice the man I ever . . ."

He couldn't finish, his last breath bubbling out of him in sad little sputters of blood and unfinished words. His eyes went glassy and Trish screamed. I held her as police officers and passersby gathered around us. Kids I knew stood among the witnesses, the girls crying, the guys trying to look manly. "Briefcase Boy," someone whispered and others took it up. As a chant swelled from the crowd: "Briefcase Boy! Briefcase Boy!" I raised a hand, shook my head, and nodded significantly toward the hysterical girl sobbing on my chest. No, not now. I looked down at her, watching in fascination as her ruby lips formed a word, a puff of perfumed breath taking flight.

"Squeegee," she said.

Back in the real world, the word set the Catman laughing and Trish giggling. "You got to accessorize, man." Catman gasped. "Get a bow tie and some of those glasses with black frames."

"A pink bow tie," Trish chirped. "With really ugly purple polka dots."

The Catman guffawed, threw an arm around Trish's waist, and off they went hip-to-hip.

Wednesday was miserable. I tried to brazen it out, but my beloved classmates were demonstrating more than their usual attention span and continued to heap abuse on me and the briefcase. The stupid thing was impervious to punishment. I wasn't.

A slender girl with long dark hair fell in beside me. Ronnie somebody. Short for Veronica? "I like you," she said.

"Huh?"

"You're different. I'm different, too. Us different people gotta stick together."

"Well, it's not that I'm trying—"

"Me. I carry this." She opened her purse to reveal a butcher knife with about a ten-inch blade. Was that blood on it? I tried to veer away, but she stayed right beside me. "People give me a hard time, and I just pull out this sucker . . ." She started hacking at the air. "And I can get preeetttty nasty when I'm upset."

"Ronnie!" We turned. Sarah Landwehr, president of the drama club, came striding toward us. "I've been looking for that knife for a week. I know you're in charge of props, but you can't just walk off with stuff."

Ronnie handed over the rubber knife with a sheepish grin. "Sorry, I was meaning to return it." She glanced at me. "I've got a real meat cleaver if you'd like to use it."

"Ignore her," Sarah said to me. "She's bats. Belfry plumb full of 'em."

Ronnie grinned at me with a well-what-can-I-say shrug of her shoulders. Now I'd started to attract crazy people. What next?

I got the answer an hour later: the Doughnut—all three hundred pounds of him—bearing down on me like the

Michelin tire man gone loco. "Hey, dweeb. What ya got there?"

"Uh, it's a briefcase, Doughnut."

"That's Mr. Doughnut to you. Haw, haw."

"Sure, Mr. Doughnut."

"Let me see." He snatched it and turned it over in his huge hands. He examined every stitch, tried every clasp, looked into every pocket. "This is pretty cool. I could carry lots of stuff in something like this."

Holy smokes! Was I about to make my first convert? If Mom and Dad could only see me now. Of course this barely sentient lump of protoplasm might not count in their eyes, but—"Well, you can buy them lots of places on the Web. If—"

"Haw, haw. Just kidding." He slapped me on the shoulder so hard I stumbled. "You gotta be a real dweeb to carry something like this. That or one of them invertebrate optimists."

"It was a birthday present," I said faintly.

"Huh?"

"It was a birthday present. From my parents. They make me carry it."

"You oughta tell 'em no. Even dweebs gotta stand up for themselves. Haw, haw." To my great and eternal surprise, he handed the briefcase back to me without first punting or punching it. "You be careful, man. Some guys around here pound on dweebs."

So, I took the Doughnut's advice. That evening before I went to bed, I wrote a note to Mom and Dad and left it with the briefcase on the hall table outside their room.

Dear Mom and Dad,
The briefcase is beautiful and very, very durable. I appreciate all the thought that went into buying it. But I don't want to carry it just now. Maybe some-day when I'm in college or have a job. But now it just doesn't fit into my life. I'm sorry if this hurts anyone's feelings, but you've always taught me to stand up for myself. And I guess that's what I'm doing now. So please store it away somewhere and trust me that this is the right decision for me right now.
Love, Chad

In the morning the briefcase was nowhere in sight.

At school a lot of kids called out to me: "Hey, where's the briefcase?" or words to that effect. But I'd practiced my answer. "I won the bet. Three days, a hundred and fifty bucks." That was pretty lame, but it seemed to work. By Friday, the attention had disappeared and I rejoined the ranks of the comfortably anonymous. "Squeegee" hadn't caught on as an epithet, and I never heard it again.

Ronnie Hainz (I'd learned her last name) dropped into the chair beside me in study hall. "I heard you won some kind of bet for carrying that briefcase."

"That was just a story. I told my parents I just didn't want to take it to school anymore."

"Good move." She hesitated. "I'm sorry about that thing with the rubber knife the other day. I was on my way to the prop room when I saw those guys giving you a hard time. And, I don't know, I just got inspired. But I didn't mean anything, you know, mean."

"It's okay," I said. "It was kind of funny."

"Good." She caught her lip in her teeth for a second and then grinned. "So now you can have a little fun, huh?" She winked at me.

"Uh, yeah," I said. "Fun would be good."

"Anyone usually sit in this seat?"

"Not really."

"Good. I think I'm going to like it here."

JERSEY DAY

Featuring:

Shauna Neumann, *feminist and lover of poetry*

Lenny Lutjens, *surprisingly sane football player (a cornerback)*

Julie "the Diesel" Cecil, *large human being*

Randy "the Doughnut" Schmidtke, *offensive tackle, enormous human being*

"Oh, look, Shauna! Lorna's got one!" Julie Cecil craned her neck, all excited because Lorna Salzwedal had found a football jersey on her homeroom desk. "Number seventy-six. That's . . ." Julie ran through numbers in her head. ". . . that's Jerry Binkowski! He's cute."

"Bing Binkowski?" I said. "Julie, he's barely a higher primate. Any dumber and he'd go on all fours."

"I think he's cute. Chubby, but cute."

Well, he was sort of cute. Not my type, but I'm openminded on the subject of cute. Still, I wasn't about to agree with Julie on Jersey Day, otherwise known as the Day the Cute Girls Get Cute Guys and All the Rest of Us Get Humiliated.

We started wrestling with our lockers, a process that can take anywhere from a few seconds to half an hour, depending on the mood of the ancient combination locks. Mine was in an ugly temper, and I gave the door an unusually vehement kick after my third failed attempt. Beside me, Julie popped her locker open, heaved in an armload of books, and turned her attention back to the drama of Jersey Day.

Let me explain this profoundly sexist tradition. Every Friday morning during football season the team has a game-day breakfast before school. Gorged and cocky, the players then have half an hour to leave their spare jerseys on the desks of their chosen females. When the doors open for the general population at 7:30, girls rush to their homerooms to see if they're among the week's lucky ones. A lot of girls might as well take their time—Julie and I are two of them—but hope blooms weekly in many a bosom and dignity is in pretty short supply around here in the half hour before homeroom.

Julie thumped me on the shoulder, causing me to flub my fifth try at the lock. "Ooohhh, look! Nancy Petrie's got one."

Despite myself, I looked. Lorna and Nancy were comparing jerseys, squealing, and hopping up and down like two kids on a trampoline.

"Fifty-four," Julie mused. "That's a linebacker's number. It's . . . ah . . . Don't tell me . . ."

"You don't have to worry about that," I growled.

"That's Steve Fiefer's number. Now, he's really cute. All that curly brown hair. Even you have to admit *he's* cute."

"He's cute, Julie. A sociopath, probably destined to spend his life in prison, but cute."

"He's just got a wild streak. And you're just jealous."

I groaned. "I won't even dignify that comment with a denial."

"Because you can't. So, ha!" Humming a bright little tune, she pushed me out of the way, spun the lock expertly, and popped open my locker. "There you go. Service with a smile."

Her little trick didn't help my mood, and I let her have it with a blast of sarcasm that surprised even me: "Julie, why are you so enamored with an emotionally destructive tradition that demeans women, provokes unseemly demonstrations of brainless-blonde ecstasy and heartbreak, glorifies a game originally played with a severed head, and no doubt leads to numerous cases of sexually transmitted disease and unwanted pregnancy? Now just why is that?"

She did her aristocratic sniff and gazed down at me from her lofty height of six-foot-one. "I think it's romantic. I like to see people happy. I think it's a nice tradition."

"It's infantile and you're hopeless."

"And you're jealous. Jealous, jealous, jealous."

"Okay, I'm jealous." I shut my locker with a kick. "Let's get to homeroom."

Usually I have to jog to keep up with Julie as the crowd parts before her. Julie is not only tall, she's built like a bulldozer. Cecil the Diesel I call her in my diary. But never to her face. The girl's got enough problems. Literary taste, for one. She plows through a six-hundred-page bodice-ripper romance and a couple of Silhouette Desires or Harlequin Temptations a week. The results are predictable. Julie sees life as this huge romance unfolding before her very eyes. Love is on the prowl everywhere she looks. That it never pounces on her doesn't discourage her a bit since today may just be the day.

I have no such illusions. Not that I don't have some assets in the physical attractiveness department, mind you. My problem is personality. Or, more exactly, attitude. To wit: I am bright, I test high, I don't hide who I am or want to be. Guys don't handle that well. Or at least none I've met. Well, too bad for them.

Okay, so maybe I'm a little on the rigid side, but Julie goes to the other extreme, flirting with every guy who'll talk to her and constantly updating her wardrobe. Wednesday afternoon she'd dragged me to a sale at Prange's. She'd tried on fourteen outfits (I counted), and I was approaching terminal boredom by the time she'd finished. I was idly examining a sheer blouse with a very low neckline when she came out of the changing room in street clothes. "Hey, good choice, Shauna. Major décolletage."

"Yeah, right," I said, hanging the blouse back on the rack. "As if I'm going to start playing those games just to get guys to look at me."

"Well, if I had your figure, I wouldn't hide it under all those frumpish clothes."

"You mean my *comfortable* clothes. And the word is *frumpy*, not *frumpish*."

"Whatever. But really, you'd look great in that. Try it on."

"No. Are we done?"

"Not until you try on that blouse."

"If I try it on can we leave then?"

"We'll see."

Grumbling, I took the blouse into the changing room. I pulled my Boundary Waters sweatshirt over my head, slipped on the blouse, buttoned the few buttons provided, and turned for a look in the mirror. Holy crap! I haven't exactly been short on bust in a couple of years, but this was positively indecent! And . . . Well, yeah, I looked pretty darned good.

"What's the holdup?" Julie called.

"Just looking it over."

"Let me see or it doesn't count."

I groaned and opened the door to give her a peek.

"Wow! You've got to buy that, Shauna."

"No way. Where would I wear it?"

"To dances. On dates."

"I don't go to dances, and I don't get dates."

"You could start. If you wore something feminine for a change, some guy might have the courage to ask you out."

"What's that supposed to mean?"

"Some clothes that didn't hide—"

"No, the courage bit."

"Well, you do scare the heck out of guys. You know that. I think you try to scare them."

"No, I don't!" I snapped, and closed the door on her.

"Yes, you do. Today you practically bit the head off that new kid in English. And just because he disagreed with you on a stupid poem."

"Emily Dickinson's poems are not stupid!"

"Okay, because he disagreed with you on a smart poem. Does that make it okay to take a guy's head off? You ought to be glad there's one guy who'll open his mouth on your favorite subject."

"Not if he's a dope," I called. I hung the blouse on its hanger and pulled on my sweatshirt.

"I thought he had a point."

"Then you're a dope."

There was a long pause before she said, "Am not. I'm going to look at purses."

Oh, crap. I was going to have to apologize or she'd torture me for the rest of the afternoon with a display of hurt feelings. I slapped on my baseball cap and went to play my part in the ritual.

It wasn't until we were having an ice cream at Minty's that she sighed and said, "Shauna, you know I love you. You're funny, you're smart, and you're kind to animals. But why do you have to crush every guy who disagrees with you? I mean, it was only English class. And Lenny doesn't seem like such a bad guy."

"Lenny?"

"Leonard Lutjens, that new kid you almost decapitated."

"I could never be interested in a guy with an alliterative name."

"So you do like him?"

"I didn't say that."

"So if you aren't interested in a guy, it's okay to rip his head off?"

"You're twisting what I meant."

"What did you mean? That you'd be interested in him if he didn't have a first and last name starting with the same letter?"

What had I meant? And why was I blushing? I never blush. I stood up abruptly. "So are we going shopping or are we just going to sit here getting fat?"

"Sounds OK to me. What's the rush?"

"I've got things to do."

"Oh, big midweek date, huh?"

"I'm leaving."

She followed, humming one of the bright little tunes

she always hums when she's hit one of my hot buttons. Okay, maybe I did like Lenny Lutjens a little bit, alliterative name or not. And maybe he wasn't a dope just because he'd totally botched the interpretation of "To hear an oriole sing." But he'd been so confident, and I hate that because I'm rarely confident about anything except poetry, no matter how I come across to people. But what am I supposed to do? Let everyone know how confused and hurt I feel when guys ignore me or snub me or just don't notice me? No way. Not even Julie gets to know that about me.

On Thursday I resolved to be patient if Lenny Lutjens opened his mouth in English. And maybe I would have been if Mrs. Ellendorf hadn't exposed my favorite Emily Dickinson poem to desecration. Mrs. Ellendorf calls "I died for beauty" one of Emily's "morbid poems," but I don't think it's morbid at all. Emily dies for beauty and is buried. Soon afterward someone who died for truth is laid next to her. They talk about how truth and beauty are the same until the moss grows over their gravestones, stopping their lips. Now *that* is romantic. (And Julie thinks I have no romance in my soul. Ha!)

As usual, no one offered an opinion. And, as usual, Mrs. Ellendorf eventually gave up on the others and turned to me. But before I could open my mouth, Lenny raised his hand. "I think it's Christ who's buried beside her. I mean, he died for truth."

Before I could think twice, I heard myself snap, "That is so stupid, I just can't believe it! How fast do you think moss grows, you dope?"

"Huh?"

"How fast does moss grow? What's the matter? Is that too tough a question?"

"Well, not fast, I guess, but I don't see—"

"The answer is *slow*. And Christ rose from the dead after three days, right?"

"Yes."

"So if it's Christ, what's he doing lying there for a year or two, talking to Emily until the moss grows over their gravestones? He'd be out founding a major religion. Or doing some miracles. Or ascending to Heaven. Or *something*. He would *not* be lying in the grave next to Emily!"

"Now, Shauna," Mrs. Ellendorf said. "There's no reason to be abusive."

I waved a hand. "I'm sorry. Stupidity makes me irritable." I glared out the window, angrier at myself than at anyone else.

Mrs. Ellendorf was mightily ticked off when she slammed the door to her office. "Shauna Neumann! I am ashamed of you! It's all well and good that you feel passionately about poetry, but that is no excuse for abusing a classmate."

"Yes, ma'am," I said. "I'm sorry."

"Don't play that humble, I'm sorry act on me! You be polite to people or you'll see your grade drop like a stone. And if you point out that's a cliché, I will resort to violence this very moment and plead temporary insanity afterward."

"Yes, ma'am. I'm sorry. I really am."

"You'd better be. Now scat! I'm sick of looking at you."

Julie was waiting for me in the hall, anxious to get the blow-by-blow. But I walked past her without a word, afraid I'd start crying if I said anything to anybody for at least an hour.

That night I had a long talk with myself. I'd made a mess of the day, ruined any chance I had with Lenny Lutjens (if I'd ever imagined having one), exasperated my favorite teacher, and been a jerk (again) in front of the class. And tomorrow was Jersey Day. The prospect was almost too much, and I considered telling Mom I was sick. But I had my pride to consider. Besides, just maybe some guy would leave a jersey on my desk. I mean, it could happen. No, it can't! the stronger, feminist side of me snapped. Now think straight. Get some fresh air.

I got a jacket and went for a long walk on the bike path a block from our house. It's not as if you're the only one, I told myself. Most girls don't get jerseys.

But that didn't help. I wasn't most girls, I was me. And it hurt never to be asked, even if Jersey Day was a lot of sexist junk.

I tried: It's not your fault if all those guys are too dumb to notice you.

But I heard Julie's voice tease, *Frumpeee clothes, sweetie. What are you hiding from?*

That's frumpish, I said, just to be contrary.

You try to scare 'em away, she teased.

No, I don't. They're just a bunch of wimps.

No. You're just a bitch.

I don't know who said that one. It wasn't Julie's voice anymore. So I guess it must have been Mrs. Ellendorf's. Or maybe Lenny's. Or maybe my own.

And at that point, darn it, I started crying.

I was okay in the morning. A little bruised but okay, the feminist side of me firmly in control. When I kicked my locker shut, Lorna Salzwedal and Nancy Petrie were still squealing and bouncing up and down like kids on a trampoline. But they were old news, and Julie was already searching out other pairings of girls, jocks, and jerseys. While she kept up a running commentary on budding and withering romances, I gave myself a pep talk: Jersey Day is a disgusting, demeaning, sexist tradition. If some moron leaves a jersey on your desk, throw it back in his face!

But the weaker part of me bleated: But suppose he's really cute?

You can't be bought with a piece of cloth! Now forget it. It's not going to happen anyway.

Randy Schmidtke, the notorious Doughnut, hove into view around the corner ahead of us, an immense equipment bag slung over his shoulder. Kids scattered like so much flotsam under the bow of a battleship. Like Julie, the Doughnut could stand to lose a few pounds, but the majority of his three-hundred-plus pounds is solid, including the mass between his ears. Recognition flickered in his dull eyes. "Hey, Julie," he rumbled. "How's it goin'?"

Julie shifted smoothly into the role of one of her

romantic heroines: the queenly statuesque type. "Why, it's kind of you to ask, Randall. Very well, thank you. And you?"

"Good. Game tonight. Gonna pound 'em."

"Oh, dear. Well, I'm happy you're keeping up with your athletic endeavors. Do have a good game."

"Yeah, thanks."

They passed like battleship and ocean liner, lesser vessels bobbing helplessly in their wakes. At the door of our homeroom, Julie paused to take a breath. "Well, here we are again, the moment of truth." She squared her shoulders and marched in.

Okay, I'll admit it. For two years now I've held my breath at this moment on every Jersey Day. Maybe that makes me a hypocrite, but I can't help it. The Friday before Homecoming last season, there'd actually been a jersey lying on my desk, and I heard myself let out a squeal. Fortunately it had been a very small squeal, which I managed to strangle in the vicinity of the epiglottis as Trish Draves snatched up the jersey and gave me a defiant glare. She finished adjusting her hair, slipped the jersey over her head, and pulled it down over her perfect chest to reveal Marvin Katt's number. She gave me a don't-you-wish stare and went back to talking to two other girls wearing jerseys.

At my shoulder, Julie had said, "Stupid bimbo. She could have put it on the windowsill if she wanted to mess with her hair."

Trish must have said something about us, because

they looked our way and giggled. I clenched my teeth and went to sit down at my desk.

But that was way back last season, and since then I've pretty much accustomed myself to disappointment. I suppose that's why this time the sight of the neatly folded jersey lying on my desk didn't register at first. But it sure did with Julie, who gripped my arm so hard I yelped. "Number eleven, that's . . . that's . . . I don't know who that is."

I approached the jersey warily, half expecting it to disappear. This just had to be a mistake. Or some kind of joke. I glanced at Julie, who was frowning so hard a line had appeared on her broad forehead. "Well, whose is it, Julie?"

"It's a quarterback number or a defensive back, maybe a kicker. . . ." Suddenly, her face brightened. "It's a defensive back, one of those whatchamacallems . . . cornerbacks. It's Lenny Lutjens's number! He doesn't play much, but I've seen him on the sidelines."

I reached out, still wary, and cautiously fingered the number eleven to make sure it wasn't fake. "What do I do now?"

"Put it on, dummy."

"I can't. It's got to be a mistake."

"No, it doesn't."

"He's giving a jersey to me? I called him a dope in class yesterday."

"Maybe he likes abuse. Hey, everybody's a little odd about something. Come on, put it on."

"I can't. I'll talk to him after English."

"Pleeeaase."

"No. And stop whining."

She went on begging, but I didn't listen.

As always, Julie and I really had to hustle to make it from gym to English in the four minutes between third and fourth period. I got to my seat just at the bell, caught my breath, and then risked a glance at Lenny Lutjens. He smiled tentatively. I pointed to the jersey in my lap and then to myself. He nodded. So it wasn't a mistake. I felt my cheeks getting warm and quickly opened my lit book to the day's assignment. I avoided looking at him for the rest of the period. Half a dozen times I told myself that I should put the jersey under my desk, but I let it lie on my lap the entire time, touching it every once in a while to assure myself that it was still there.

I didn't even follow the discussion, which seemed to go surprisingly well without my help. I suppose most people thought I was pouting, but I was too distracted to think about poetry. What was I going to do? I had to give the jersey back. That much I knew. I couldn't be a part of something as sexist as Jersey Day. No way. But suddenly the romantic side of my personality exerted itself.

Why not way? she snapped, catching my feminist side completely off guard.

Well, to begin with, it glorifies a macho sport.

And so what? This is an American high school in the fall. Guys play football. Girls cheer. Go with it and enjoy.

But guys don't choose girls to wear their jerseys on the basis of intelligence or competence or accomplishment, they just choose on looks.

That's reverse sexism. What's true for many isn't necessarily true for all. And don't forget personality. There are some not-so-great-looking girls wearing jerseys.

But why me then? I mean, I called Lenny a—

Ask him.

It's a trick. He's trying to buy me off.

Weak argument. Talk to him.

I'm frightened.

Okay, don't talk to him. Be miserable all your life.

I'll call him on the phone tonight.

He'll be playing football, chicken.

I'll call him tomorrow.

That'll be too late.

But—

Bwaaak, puck, puck, puck. Bwaaak, puck, puck, puck.

Just then Julie passed me a note. I opened it, expecting more of her nagging. But the unfamiliar handwriting read: "Want to meet for lunch in the cafeteria?"

I looked over at Lenny and managed to nod. I bet he wants the jersey back, I thought. Heck, he's probably been thinking, too.

"Can I sit with you?" Julie asked.

"Are you out of your mind? Of course not."

"Just offering moral support."

"Odd coming from you."

She stuck out her tongue at me and went off to find another friend to sit with. I hesitated a moment and then set off resolutely for the place across from Lenny.

"Hi," he said. "Went for the salad instead of the cheeseburger, huh?"

"Their cheeseburgers scare me. Besides, I'm trying to lose a few pounds."

"You look fine to me." He took a big bite of cheeseburger.

I took a breath. "So, do you want it back?"

"What?"

"The jersey."

"No. What makes you think that? Hey, are you going to eat standing up?"

I plopped myself down. "Okay, I need to know what the deal is."

He shrugged. "Nothing too hard to figure out. I'd like you to wear my jersey, cheer for me at the game, and meet me afterward for a pizza. Or a burger or a salad if you don't like pizza."

"I like pizza fine. Why?"

"Well, I wouldn't want you eating something you didn't like."

Are you being purposely dense? I bit my lip. "No, I meant, why do you want to go out with me?"

"Why not?"

"To begin with, I called you a dope in class yesterday."

He shrugged. "That was just about poetry. I didn't worry about it."

On a normal day I might have decapitated him right then and there. I mean, poetry is the distillation of culture, of all human striving. It is . . . I took a breath. Steady. He's just a guy eating a cheeseburger. At least he's bipedal and doesn't drool. "I didn't know you played football."

"I don't make a big deal of it. And I don't play a lot since there are a couple of pretty good seniors ahead of me. But Hal Eckhart is a little banged up, so I'll probably play most of tonight's game."

"Julie told me you're some kind of defensive player."

"A cornerback. Do you know much about football?"

"Not really."

"Cornerbacks play out on the edge of the defense. We turn in running plays and try to keep receivers from catching the ball. Do the job, nobody notices. Screw up, everybody does. But at least we spend most of the time running away from where really big people are beating on each other."

"Sounds sane to me."

"That's what my mom says. . . . So, is it a deal? You wear the jersey, I'll try not to make you ashamed of the number, and afterward we'll go out for pizza?"

I hesitated. "I'm not sure. I mean, I never thought anyone would give me one, so I always thought I'd have the courage to give it back if somebody did give me one. A jersey, that is. Not a pizza."

He frowned. "I don't think I followed that."

"Never mind. Okay, it's a deal." I jumped up and headed for the garbage cans to dump my untouched salad. And maybe throw up. But I managed not to do that.

Julie was lurking outside the cafeteria. "Well, what'd he say?"

"I'm supposed to wear his jersey, cheer for him at the game, and go out with him for pizza afterward."

"And what'd you say?"

I set my books on the floor. "I said okay. Here, help me get this on."

Together we wrestled the jersey over my head and sweatshirt. Tight fit. Lenny wasn't exactly your big guy. I looked down at the big number eleven stretched across my chest, then looked up to see Julie's eyes filling with tears.

"Oh, Julie. I'm sorry. I'll take it off. I'll give it back to him."

"Don't you dare! I'm okay. It's just that you look so darned beautiful. I'm just . . . just really happy for you."

"But—"

"No! You give it back to him and I'll never speak to you again. Or at least not for a month. Or a week. No, definitely a month at least."

"Julie, it'll happen for you. Maybe next—"

She shook her head violently. "No, it won't happen for me! I know what I look like. I know you call me Cecil the Diesel in your diary."

"You peeked!"

"Of course I peeked! You would too if I was stupid enough to leave my diary where anyone could pick it up."

"Julie, that name was just a joke."

"Oh, I don't care about the stupid name. But don't tell me I'm going to get a jersey one of these weeks because I'm not. But I'm fine. I'm okay. I'll see you at the game. We'll cheer like heck for Lenny." She hurried off, wiping at her eyes.

It may sound odd, but I'd never fantasized beyond finding a jersey on my desk. So I was surprised when girls I hardly knew spoke to me that afternoon, congratulated me, asked where Lenny and I were going after the game. And it was fun, darn it.

I met Julie at the stadium, and we found seats in the student section. I sat down, carefully arranged my seat cushion and lap robe, blew on my cup of cocoa, and prepared to analyze the game of football. All that was before I realized no one in the student section sits during a game. As soon as the game started, people were on their feet, yelling, screaming, shouting instructions, and generally making a *lot* of noise. So much for my plans. I got up and tried to get an idea of what was going on. Fortunately Julie had a radio tuned to the game and that helped some. Otherwise I was pretty much on my own since Julie was too busy screaming to explain anything.

From what Lenny had said, I didn't expect him to be smashing into other people much, but it seemed that every other play ended with him in the middle of a big pile of bodies. And every time I held my breath, hoping he'd come out of the pile alive. And every time he did, bouncing up and jogging back to the huddle, wearing a big grin. A couple of times the radio announcers mentioned his name, saying he was filling in well for Hal Eckhart. Julie nudged me hard, and a couple of girls in front of us turned around to give me fives. And I gave them back. I mean, what the heck. Might as well get with all the customs, no matter how primitive.

With three minutes to go in the game, Argyle was leading by a touchdown and something called a safety. (I hadn't seen anything safe all night.) Anyway, it added up to nine points, and everyone was pretty relaxed. But Rothburg High scored on a long pass and kicked a point, and we were only ahead by two. Then everybody got very worked up when the Rothburg kicker just tapped the ball a few yards, a lot of players piled on top of one another, and one of their guys came away with the ball. Which wasn't at all good. Or so I gathered from the cries of outrage and mortal agony coming from the crowd around me.

I yelled at Julie over the commotion: "Was that fair? I mean, can they do that?"

"Yes," she shouted. "It's called an onside kick."

Oh. Well, anyway, Rothburg tried running the ball once and then passing it a couple of times. But our guys stopped them. Everybody in the stands was screaming. Heck, I was screaming. Rothburg called a time-out to talk things over.

"It's fourth down and they'll have to pass," Julie yelled at me. "This might be Lenny's chance to be a hero."

"I just want him to get out of this alive. I mean, I hardly know him yet."

The teams lined up, and everybody in the stands started yelling again. I had Julie's radio plastered against my ear, trying to hear the broadcast. Then even the radio announcer went nuts: "Rothburg has a receiver loose in the middle of the field! He's going to be wide open! Ball's in the air. He's got it— No! Knocked away at the last second. Holy smokes, where'd Lutjens come from?"

The other announcer answered: "He came from the right cornerback spot, Gene. The free safety bit on the play-action fake, but Lutjens saw the middle open up, broke off his own coverage, and flew across the field to get a hand in to break up the pass. I don't know how he did it. Man, that was a long way. That young man has some extra fuel in his jets tonight."

"You're right on that, Dale," the first announcer said. "Just an amazing play. Anyway, the ball goes over to Argyle on downs with a minute twenty to go. If we can hold on to the ball, this one will go into the win column."

"Do you understand what happened?" I shouted to Julie.

"Lenny's a hero! I told you he would be."

And he sure seemed to be. A lot of people on the sidelines were slapping him on the back and giving him hugs. For a second he seemed to look my way, a broad grin on his face. But maybe that was just my imagination.

Like all the other girls in jerseys, I stood around in the parking lot waiting for the players to come out of the locker room. The feminist side of me grumbled a little about that, but Lenny was one of the first out, making me feel better. We gave two other couples a ride to Pizza Maestro, and it wasn't until we found chairs at the foot of a long table that I was able to tell him: "Great game."

He smiled. "Thanks. I got lucky on that last play. The receiver should have caught that ball, but I just got the tips of my fingers on it."

"It was real exciting. The radio announcers said a lot of nice things about you."

"Hey, once in a career. Got my fifteen seconds of fame."

"It's supposed to be fifteen minutes."

"Not for cornerbacks."

I guess I hadn't understood that we were meeting two dozen other people for pizza. I'd pictured a quiet Italian place, low lighting, romantic music, a candle burning in an empty Chianti bottle. You know. Maybe my disappointment showed a little bit because Lenny shouted to me over the din: "Do you want to get our own table? We could do that."

I shook my head. "No, if this is the tradition, I'll go with it."

Anyway, there was a lot of yelling and laughter and kidding around. Lots of people I sort of knew were there, all surprisingly normal, though I don't suppose a one of them gave a rap about Emily Dickinson. But I guess that *is* normal. Ken Bauer had this routine about his buddy Rollin Acres and Rollin's girlfriend, Sandy Dunes, buying a golf course to go with their names. And Ronnie Hainz, one of the student trainers, brought out a really gross rubber butcher's knife to cut the pizza, and . . . Oh, I don't know. A lot of it was funnier at the time than it seemed later. For a while the Doughnut sat on the other side of me. He didn't say much, just grinned and inhaled pizza by the slab. After he left I asked Lenny, "Where'd the Doughnut go?"

"Home. He never stays long. Doughnut's not quite what people think. Pretty quiet, really."

Really. I never would have guessed. Perhaps . . . but, no, that'd never work. Anyway, I enjoyed myself until I started getting a headache. I tried to ignore it, but before long it turned into one of those pulsing-brain-tumor sort of headaches that make you want to throw up. "You okay?" Lenny asked.

"Just got a headache."

"Want to go? Things are about to break up here anyway."

"Okay."

I was hoping the fresh air would make me feel better, but the headache was thudding like a hammer by the time we pulled up in front of my house. "Are you okay?" he asked.

I managed to nod. "I'm sorry. Just too much noise and excitement and yelling, I guess. This isn't my typical Friday. Usually, I sit home and read a book."

"Sounds kind of dull."

Yeah. Yeah, it is. "I've got to know," I said. "I'm sorry, but I've really just got to know."

"Know what?"

"Why you gave me the jersey."

"I thought we'd covered that."

"But why me? I haven't been nice to you, I'm not very good looking, and I don't fit in with your crowd. So why me?"

"I don't agree with any of that. You're the one who keeps coming up with reasons."

"I called you a dope."

"I'm used to it. I've got three older sisters."

I looked down at my lap, afraid I might start crying at any second. "You're not really a dope, you know."

"See? That's nice. I knew I was right about you."

Him saying that left me with two options: start crying or take strong action. I opted for number two, grabbed him by the back of the collar, pulled him to me, and kissed him hard on the lips. "If I'm coming down with the plague, you're dead."

"I'll take my chances."

I kissed him a second time, letting it linger for a moment, then broke it off. "You know, any relationship with me is going to take a lot of work. I am not your easy-to-get-along-with person."

"I'm your guy. Work never scared me."

Then you are really brave or really a dope. But that was only what I could have said. "Call me tomorrow, huh?"

"You can count on it."

I don't think short stories are supposed to have epilogues, but this one does. I saw quite a bit of Lenny that

next week, but I still held my breath when I followed
Julie into homeroom that Friday. No need, his spare jersey—a black home jersey this time—lay folded neatly on
my desk. Julie immediately did an about-face and marched
down the hall. "Julie," I called. "Julie, wait."

She ignored me. The Doughnut came around the corner just then, lugging his equipment bag as always. Julie
stopped right in front of him, hands on her hips. "Randall, do you have your spare jersey in there?"

"Uh, yeah."

"I want it. Give!" She held out an imperious hand.

He set down his equipment bag meekly, dug out his
spare jersey, and handed it to her. "Thank you, Randall,"
she said. "I'll see you after the game. Don't get hurt."

"Okay. Yell loud so I can hear you when I'm playing.
I'd like that."

I ran back to homeroom, grabbed my jersey, and
joined Julie in the girls' restroom. I helped her on with
the Doughnut's jersey. "Don't say a thing," she said. "I
know he's kind of fat and not real bright. But he's train-
able."

"Actually, I think there may be more to him than you
think."

Julie studied herself in the mirror. "There may be to
us all. I think there just may be. . . . Come on. I have
been waiting *years* for this."

BIG CHICAGO

Featuring:
Jeremy "Big Chicago" Stachowiak,
    linebacker
Howie Burlingame, *small kid*
Gangsta wannabes
Sarah Landwehr, *sensible person*
Rebecca "Becks" Campbell, *kicker and
    speaker of the King's English*

I 'd had a good practice Wednesday afternoon, and I expected Coach Carlson to compliment me when he called me into his office. Instead, he was sorting deficiency reports into neat piles on his desk. "Sit down, Chicago. Seems we've got a problem. Three deficiencies. That's a lot."

This again. "Yeah, well, it's not as bad as all that, Coach. You know, new school. I'm adjusting. I'll get my grades up."

He sorted papers. "English, history, and chemistry. All with the same box checked: Doesn't apply himself."

"I've never been that great a student, Coach."

"Which class is the biggest problem?"

I shrugged. They were all problems. School was a problem. As in I didn't give a rat's butt. I wanted to play football, wrestle, and maybe go out for baseball if I was still eligible come spring.

"Well, come on, Chicago. We've got to start somewhere. You've got two weeks to lift two of three deficiencies, or I'm going to have to sit you down. Those are the rules."

"Just two weeks? In my old school, deficiencies didn't count that much, just grades at quarter and semester."

"Different rules here. Two weeks. We play this week on Thursday, and I'll need confirmation that you're making progress by a week from Friday. That's my deadline."

"But that's not even two weeks!"

"*My* deadline, Chicago. The *team's* deadline. So you

can play tomorrow night, but that'll be it unless you get your act together."

I stared at my hands.

"So," he said, "grades were a problem at your old school, too?"

I shrugged.

He stared at me. "Look, Chicago, being evasive isn't going to help here. Now I'm pleased with the way you're playing. We were weak at linebacker, and you've filled a big hole for us. But unless you get your grades up, you sit. Period."

I nodded, already feeling the season slipping away from me. "Okay, Coach."

"So what are you going to do?"

"Study more, I guess."

"Think that'll do it?"

Not unless I suddenly began to care. "Not much else to do."

"I'll talk to your teachers. My bet is that chemistry is going to be your biggest challenge. Anybody can pass history and English if they listen in class."

It's those little squiggly things called commas, Coach. And the dots and double dots and dots and squiggles. That and not knowing how to spell more than twenty or thirty short words. As in: *I, could, give, a, rat's,* and *butt.* "If you think it'll do any good," I said.

"It can't hurt. But don't expect any breaks just because you play football. I don't work that way, and I don't ask other teachers to work that way. It's up to you."

"Yes, sir."

"Okay. Get out of here. Tell the Doughnut to come in. He's got two." I slid out the door. "And study!" he shouted after me.

Yeah, right. I told the Doughnut to go in for his whipping, grabbed my gym bag, and headed for the halls. Crap. Even the Doughnut had fewer deficiencies than I did.

I was bummed. Big time. I could try to study. If Mom had unpacked the dictionary, I could start looking up all the words five letters and longer. I could even tell myself that I cared if I graduated or not. But I didn't. Never had. Mom and Dad hadn't graduated from high school. Mom got a G.E.D. later, and she's tried to make me care about school. Dad never gave a rap. Or at least he hadn't the last time I'd seen him. I doubt that the jerk has changed his mind.

Three gangsta wannabes had a little scrawny kid hedged up against the lockers. I didn't know the kid and I didn't know any of them, but I pushed in anyway. "You guys got a problem with my buddy here?" I growled.

They backed off a little. The tall guy who seemed to be the leader said, "We were just giving him a little gas, Chicago. What's it to you?"

So they knew who I was. "Ain't nothing to me 'cept it seems there's three against one."

"Ain't three against one. Ain't nobody against—"

"Don't you think I can count to three?"

He hesitated. "Well, sure. But—"

"So beat it or let's take it outside. One, two, three of

you, I don't care. I'll give you some practice counting lumps."

They looked at one another. "We got no fight with you, Chicago. We don't got no fight with him. We were just having a little fun."

"Okay. You've had it. Now beat it before I start having some of my own. *Comprende,* maggots?"

They backed off, turned, and headed down the hall. The scrawny kid didn't wait to thank me, just scuttled off in the opposite direction. No matter. I hadn't done it for him. I'd wanted to kick some butt, and the gangsta wannabes fit my priorities just right. . . . A week from Friday. I was dead. I might as well quit school and save myself the pain. Except that I couldn't because I wasn't eighteen, and here in the sticks somebody might actually come looking for me. Next stop, alternative school—no sports, skaggy babes, and an agonizing death by boredom.

A piece of paper lay folded on my homeroom desk Thursday morning. I opened it, expecting to find a note from Coach Carlson, my counselor, or one of my teachers. Instead, it read: "Thanks for saving my life yesterday. Howie Burlingame." I hadn't even thought about the incident since then, and it took me a second to connect the name. Well, I hadn't exactly saved his life, although with a name like Howie it was a wonder the kid had survived this long. I crumpled the note and tossed it in the wastebasket.

Howie might not have had many buddies, but the story was out anyway. Several people asked me about it that morning. I told them the truth: I'd just felt like kicking some gangsta butt.

"Were you in a gang in Chicago?" one girl asked me.

"No."

"Did you know anybody who was?"

"Yeah, sure. I guess. Most of them were just like here: wannabes."

"If I lived in a big city, I'd join a gang."

"Why?"

"I don't know. Because then somebody's always got your back, I guess."

"Why are you so worried about your back?"

"Well, you know, big city, lots of crime. I wouldn't want to be robbed or raped or anything. Better to be in a gang."

I shook my head. These kids. "It's just a city," I said. "You live with it, it lives with you. Stay away from trouble, it stays away from you."

"But I always heard . . ." She babbled on, but I'd lost interest. I made a show of opening my English book, though reading some stupid short story was nearly as bad as listening to the babble.

I hadn't gotten halfway through the story by class and flunked the quiz I'd known was coming. Five questions, true or false. Probably half the kids hadn't read the story, but most of them must have been better guessers or better cheaters.

Ms. Halston handed back our essays from the week before for revision and then corrected the quizzes while we looked over her comments. I stared at the D minus at the top of mine and then at the maze of red circles, inserted punctuation, and various abbreviations that probably meant something if you cared to look them up in the student guide. I didn't.

I glanced up just in time to see Ms. Halston reach what must have been my quiz. Her red pen slashed at my answers. She shook her head, made a mark in her grade book, and then stared at me. "See me after class, Jeremy," she said. A few of the girls and a couple of the guys giggled. I scowled at them. *Careful.* You do not want to do that real loud right now.

The class dragged through to its dismal conclusion. I tried to stay awake. But concentrating on the discussion was more than I could manage. When the bell rang, I made for the door, thinking maybe she'd forgotten about talking to me. "Jeremy," she snapped. "Sit!"

I sat.

After the rest of the class had filed out, she opened her grade book and studied a page. "Coach Carlson called me last night. Told me that you wanted to do better in this class. That you were prepared to turn over a new leaf. The answers on your quiz don't indicate that."

"I, uh, concentrated on a couple of other things last night and kind of forgot about the short story."

"Lame excuse. If you want to get your deficiency lifted and play football, I would suggest you don't forget again."

"Yes, ma'am." She closed her grade book and started shuffling papers. I was about to ask her if I could go when she said: "I heard you broke up a fight in the hall yesterday."

"Well, it wasn't really a fight. Just three guys giving a smaller kid a hard time. I didn't like the odds." Actually, *I* was the one trying to pick a fight, lady. They just didn't oblige.

"That was still a nice thing to do. I don't know you well, Jeremy, but I get the impression your heart's in the right place. But you need to get going in this class. I don't hand out passing grades to people just because they do a good deed now and then. Or play football. You need to read the assignments, pass the tests, and—particularly in your case—learn to use the dictionary once in a while."

"Yes, ma'am."

"All right then. Read your assignment. I expect you to do better on the next quiz."

"Yes, ma'am."

Yes, ma'am. Yes, ma'am. Yes, ma'am. Yes, sir. Yes, sir. Yes, sir. Coach had done his work, and my history and chemistry teachers told me pretty much the same stuff. Mr. Everett also brought up the business with the Howie kid, describing it as a "mugging." I corrected him, wishing that everyone would just forget about it. I mean, even if I'd done a good thing for the wrong reasons, it wasn't a big deal.

I haven't made a lot of friends in the school yet, so as usual I sat by myself at lunch. I was concentrating on my food when the three gangsta wannabes took the bench across from me. "Hey, Chicago," the leader said.

"Hey," I said.

"How you doin'?"

"Okay." I kept eating, not bothering to make eye contact.

"Well, we're taking some crap about that business yesterday. Assistant principal had us up in his office yelling at us for half an hour this morning."

"Why you telling me?"

"Because we wondered how he knew. Wondered if you'd gone up and squealed."

"Be careful," I said. "There are a few words you don't want to use around me."

"So it was you then?"

"Nope. I didn't waste another minute thinking about you jerks."

"Then it must have been that Howie kid," another one of them said. "Now we should *really* get him."

"Shut up, you jerk," the leader snapped, proving that we agreed on at least one thing. I'd try *maggot* again, see if I could get a second on that one, too.

They sat for a moment, not saying anything. I started eating my Jell-O. "Look, Chicago," the leader said. "We don't want any trouble with you. But squealing ain't never cool. We were just having a little fun, and now that Howie kid's got us in serious crap."

"That's not my problem."

"Yeah, but we need to talk to that kid. We won't hurt him, just—you know—explain the picture."

"Makes no difference to me what you do."

"That's what we wanted to hear." They started to get up.

I ran the spoon around the bowl, swallowed the last of the Jell-O, and looked up. "Speaking of pictures, maybe you'd like to have a look at this one. I've been in kind of a bad mood recently. You know, feeling like it'd be really good to pound somebody. So if I hear you're giving that kid any crap, I'll come looking for you. *Comprende,* maggots?"

"You know," said the kid who'd shot off his mouth earlier, "if you didn't have your football buddies, somebody might try to close that mouth of yours."

I looked around. "I don't see any of them. That must mean I'm supposed to be scared now."

They glared at me and stomped off.

We were playing on Thursday instead of Friday for reasons nobody had bothered to explain to me. I was ready. Boy, was I ready. If this was going to be my last game, I was going to make good and sure that people remembered Chicago.

I had one great game. Twice I hit the running back so hard he coughed up the ball. Two or three times I forced the quarterback into bad passes. Then, with the game on the line in the fourth quarter, I sacked him on two consecutive plays. Everybody could take their stupid deficiency reports and cram them; I would be missed out there.

A lot of parents and students came onto the field after the game. People slapped me on the shoulder, and I heard: "Great game, Chicago" more times than I could count. Mom was there near the stands. "Good job, baby. You really had them running from you."

I grinned, because—what the heck—I had a right to

enjoy this. From the stands, I heard a voice shout, "Hey, fifty-seven." I looked for the voice, spotted this small, skinny guy, not that much bigger than the scrawny kid who stood beaming at his side. I walked over, Mom trailing a little behind, her face suddenly worried. The skinny guy stuck out his hand. "John Burlingame. My boy told me what you did for him yesterday. I'm grateful. So's his mother. It's great to hear about some of you big guys standing up for us little guys." He grinned and hugged Howie to his side.

Howie had some kind of speech problem, stuttering a little to get out, "Th-th-this is Chicago, Pop. Big Chicago. He says we're buddies."

"Well, you're big, Chicago. And I don't mean just your size."

I shrugged. "Well, it was three against—" But before I could finish, the crowd started sweeping them away toward the exits.

"Thanks again," the guy yelled.

I waved.

"What'd you do, baby?" Mom asked.

"Oh, I just chased off three gangsta wannabes that were giving that kid a hard time. It was three against one, and I was kinda in a bad—"

She linked her arm in mine. "Don't make excuses. That was a very nice thing to do. I'm proud of you. I think this move is going to work out for us."

By morning some of the shine was off the game for me. I took a couple of Tylenol for my bruises and headed for school. Well, at least I'd managed to read the stupid short story for English before falling asleep. In the hall outside the administration office, a tall blonde girl came up to me and stuck out a hand. "Chicago, I'm Sarah Landwehr," she said, demonstrating a fair amount of muscle behind the handshake.

"Yeah, I've seen you around."

"I heard what you did for Howie Burlingame. That was nice."

"Yeah, well—"

"Do you know his story?"

"Uh, no. Not really."

"He's autistic. He didn't speak until he was eight. For enjoyment he goes to the library after school and copies long lists from the almanac. He's got notebooks full of just numbers."

"Oh. Is he getting help for the whatever you called it?"

"Yes, he works with the special education teacher, and a few of us keep an eye on him."

"Well . . . that's great." I felt like shaking my head in wonder. I'd wanted to beat the crap out of somebody, anybody, and now here I was the defender of the mentally challenged.

"He doesn't talk to many people, but he talks to me. He told me how you said he was your buddy."

"I don't even know the kid. It was just three against one, and I didn't like the odds."

"You said it, and he believes it. That's what counts."

"I really don't want to be the kid's protector or anything."

"Oh, don't worry about that. He won't impose on you. That's not his way."

"So you were the one who spread the story around, huh?"

"I didn't spread it around. I just told a few decent people who don't like to see him picked on. And I told Mr. Mathias, the assistant principal, about it. I don't believe all that junk about squealing. If I see or hear about something that's not right, I tell the people who can do something about it."

I hesitated. I'd never thought about it that way, although I wasn't quite sure why. "Maybe you should let him know that those guys are talking about getting Howie."

"How do you know that?"

I told her.

"Maybe you should tell him."

"I don't know . . . I never played that game before."

She snorted. "It's not a game. People have rights. It doesn't matter if they happen to be young or just not very big. If you saw a five-year-old being abused you'd tell somebody, wouldn't you?"

"Sure."

"So what's the difference? Because he's a teenager Howie's lost his rights? I don't think so. He's got the same right to protection as anybody else. And if those kids 'get him,' as you put it, I'll make sure they pay."

"I told them I'd give them more bruises than they could count."

She stared at me. "I'm not saying what you did the other day was wrong. I'm glad you stepped in. But you ought to keep the bruises on the football field. One of those kids might be scared enough of you to start carrying a gun or a knife."

I shrugged. "Maybe you're right."

The bell rang for homeroom. "So," she said, "are you going to go tell Mr. Mathias about those kids threatening to 'get' Howie, or am I?"

"You take care of it this time. I've got to chew on some of this for a while."

"Chicken," she said, then laughed. "You're okay, Chicago. A bit of a muscle-headed jock, but you've got promise."

"Thanks," I said. "I guess."

"You've got study hall third period?"

"Yeah."

"Come down to room twenty. We run the literary magazine out of there. I know a couple of people who can help you with those deficiency reports. Still have that essay you've got to revise?"

"How do you know about that?"

"Oh, I have my sources." She laughed. "Ms. Halston is our adviser. I do some typing for her. You're just one on a list. Let me have a look at your essay, and we can knock it in shape third hour."

I dug it out of a folder and handed it to her. She started for the office door.

"Uh, Sarah," I said. She turned. "Would you like to hang out sometime? Like, you know, go out for a soda or go to a movie together?"

She made a face, the corner of her mouth turned up

in a twisted smile. "Well, Chicago, I've kind of got a thing with Kenny Bauer."

"The tight end?"

"The same."

"I've laid a couple of licks on him."

"So he's said. So, thanks, but no thanks. But come to room twenty. You've got friends there."

Not that I knew of, but after surviving the first two periods, I went. I mean, she already had my essay, and I had to have something for English class.

Sarah was busy on a computer, the room bustling with people. "Hey, Chicago," she yelled. "Talk to Becks. She's got your essay. She actually speaks and writes real English."

I thought I recognized the solid-looking, dark-haired girl who looked up from a long table. "Greetings, fellow émigré," she said. "Take a seat."

The English accent tipped me off. The football team's female kicker. She stuck out a hand. "I'm from London. It's good to meet someone else who didn't grow up in this benighted corner of the colonies."

This was all a little too fast for me. *Benighted?* "Hi. Uh, you kick pretty good."

"Actually, I kick pretty well. But we'll talk about that distinction later. I heard how you broke up that fight. That was nice. I might just have started flailing on those cretins to work off some frustration."

Flailing? Cretins? "Well, I felt like it, but things didn't work out that way."

"Lucky for them. So . . ." She held up my essay.

"Excuse me for being blunt, but do you ever consult a dictionary?"

"Not very often."

"It shows. Your spelling is execrable. But we'll worry about that later, too. Your punctuation isn't too bad. I deciphered how you do it, and you're not that far off. You just need to learn a couple of tricks. As in, recognizing what is a complete sentence and what isn't."

"Okay. I guess I could handle that."

"Good. We'll start there. By the way, I play rugby, but that's something we can talk about later, too."

"Uh, when are we going to do all this talking?"

"You can start by taking me to the dance tonight if you don't have other plans. Now look here. Where you say . . ."

THE GHOST of MUM-MUM

Featuring:
Shauna Neumann, *fan of a particular football player*
Lenny Lutjens, *cornerback and irritatingly nice guy*
Julie Cecil, *overly enthusiastic fan*
Selma Rohde, *tintinnabulary fan*

M om had a late showing in Wausau; I had the dishes and Selma. As usual, Selma didn't lift a finger to help, just sat on the couch watching while I washed, rinsed, and wiped. I glanced at the clock for the twentieth time in the last five minutes. Come on, Mom; get home! I've got a life, remember? As in a date with a guy who plays football on Friday nights? So let's move it!

"Your mom's not home yet," Selma announced in her customary shrill.

"Nope."

"I wonder why she's so late."

"She's trying to sell a house."

"That'd be good if she sold a house. Really good."

"Yep," I said, dumping more dishes into the sink. How had three of us dirtied so many dishes in a day, anyway?

Selma fidgeted, trying to figure out how to continue the conversation. "Are you excited about the game?"

"Uh-huh."

"Is Lenny going to play?"

"Uh-huh."

"I like him. He's cute."

"Yep."

"When does the game start?"

"Seven o'clock."

"That's soon." Selma screwed up her face in concentration as she studied the clock. "Just twenty-five minutes," she announced proudly.

I glanced at the clock again, my fingers choosing that

precise moment to fumble a dinner plate. Enter New-ton's first law of gravity: Dropped, plates fall, breaking into a million, gazillion pieces. Or words to that effect.

"Shucks! Shucks! Shucks!" I yelped. (See above on words to that effect.)

Selma giggled. "You dropped a plate, huh?"

"Yes, I dropped a plate."

"I won't tell."

"It was an old plate, Selma. No big deal." I got out the broom and dustpan and started sweeping up shards of china.

Selma was almost bouncing off the couch in her ex-citement. "I won't tell your mom, Shauna. Really, I won't. It can be our secret."

You're not supposed to scream at the mentally handi-capped or the terminally stupid, so I took a deep, calm-ing breath. "It's really not a big deal, Selma. Mom doesn't get upset about little accidents."

"It can be our secret."

"Sure, Selma. Our secret."

She giggled and hugged herself with glee. "Our se-cret. Just you and me, right?"

"Sure, Selma. Just you and me."

Okay. Want to guess how old Selma is? Four? Five? Maybe seven? Try fifty-three. That's right, fifty-three.

Selma is Mom's cousin. Until last March, she lived in Springfield, Illinois, with her mother, my great-aunt Melba, known to everyone in the family as Mum-Mum. Twice a year Mom and I would drive down to see them for a few days. That was, believe me, quite enough. Selma is irritating; Great-Aunt Melba was a harpy. Everything in her house had to be perfect, including visiting great-nieces.

A few hours into our last visit, Mom went upstairs to take a nap. Selma was watching a quiz program in the living room, and Great-Aunt Melba was in the kitchen beating a pot roast into submission. So I figured it was safe to take an hour for some escapist literature. I curled up in an easy chair in the den and was enjoying a particularly steamy scene in Ann Rice's *Interview with a Vampire* when Great-Aunt Melba materialized at my elbow. "*What* are you doing, young lady?" she shrieked.

Now I am not a person easily startled. I do not scream during horror movies, though I have been known to moan pitifully and try to crawl under my seat. Nor am I inclined to jump when someone sneaks up on me. But Great-Aunt Melba's shriek lifted me a good foot out of the chair and short-circuited my usually acute command of verbal give and take.

"Well?"

"Uh . . . reading?" Why had I made it a question? Of course I was reading. Or had been.

"With your feet on the furniture?"

"Well, I don't have my shoes on."

"And suppose some strange man came in here and saw you?"

"Strange man?"

"Well, just look at you: barefoot, sweatshirt, jeans. Is that any way to greet guests?"

"But—"

"And your posture! Why you look like some slovenly hillbilly girl from the Ozarks."

"What's wrong with the O—" I started, but her hand snapped out like a mongoose going for a cobra and snatched the paperback out of my hands. "Zarks," I finished.

"And this . . . this book. Why you should be reading good books. Like *My Friend Flicka* or *The Good Earth*, not this trash."

"But it's not trash. Ann Rice is . . ." Well, maybe a little trashy, but . . .

"We'll just see what your mother has to say about all this trashy behavior. But in the meantime, keep your feet off my furniture!" She stalked out with my book screeching in her talons. (Make that *claws*. I think mongeese have claws.)

I always figured Great-Aunt Melba read the steamy parts before returning my book to Mom near the end of our visit. In the meantime, I'd been a good girl, voicing none of my fantasies about strangling Selma's darling Mum-Mum in her sleep. But on the trip home I announced that no way was I ever going back. Not in a hundred years.

It turned out to be more like two weeks. We were eating supper when the call came summoning us back to Springfield. Mom answered, listened, said "thank you," and hung up. She brushed away a couple of tears.

"What is it, Mom?"

"That was your Great-Aunt Melba's lawyer. She died in her sleep last night."

"Wow," I said. "I didn't think anything could kill Mum-Mum except maybe a—" I was going to say a sharpened stake or a silver bullet, but at that point my eyes filled with tears and I couldn't go on. What a wimp. I wasn't sorry she'd croaked; I hated the old bat. *That should be mongoose,* my interior editor complained. *Oh, shut up,* I snapped.

It wasn't until later that evening while we were packing to go to Springfield that I thought to ask Mom why it'd taken the lawyer all day to call.

Mom bit her lip. "Selma didn't realize her mother was dead. She thought she was just sleeping late. It wasn't until the middle of the afternoon that she called anyone."

I shook my head. "Wow. I didn't think even she was that stupid."

"Shauna, please be kind. This is going to be very hard on Selma. She's lost her mother, and now she'll have to move all the way up here."

"Say, *what?*" I yelped.

"Well, she can't live by herself. She'll have to come live with us."

"But you're only a cousin, Mom! Let social services find someplace for her. A home for the really stupid or something."

"Now, Shauna, I asked you to be kind."

"I am kind. Twice a year I'm kind for a whole week."

"Sometimes we're asked to do more."

"By whom? I didn't hear anyone asking."

Mom turned back to her packing. "You know what I mean. Now go finish getting your things together. I'm almost ready."

I won't go into all the funeral stuff. Maybe two dozen people came to the service. Then the three of us and the minister followed the hearse up to the cemetery to plant Mum-Mum's mortal remains next to those of long-dead (escaped?) Great-Uncle Hank.

I was surprised how well Selma took everything. She pointed to the marker next to the grave. "That's where my daddy's buried," she told me. "Isn't it nice they'll be together again?"

"Sure, Selma," I said.

"Real nice. You know, like they're sleeping."

I nodded. Damn it, why was I crying again?

Selma put an arm around my shoulder. "It's okay, Shauna. Mum-Mum was real old. She's up in Heaven with my daddy and the baby Jesus now."

I bit my lip, afraid I might start bawling or laughing. Would dear old daddy be the first soul ever to flee Heaven in disguise?

We spent the rest of that week packing up the house and arranging Great-Aunt Melba's affairs. On Friday, Mom and Selma went with the family lawyer to court, where Mom was appointed Selma's legal guardian. If the proceeding had contained the bit about: "If anyone here knows any reason why these two should not be joined . . ." I would have started waving both hands. But I was left back at the house, lugging about a gazillion pounds of old newspapers and magazines from the basement to the curb.

I suppose I should hand it to Selma for being a trouper. She didn't so much as shed a tear or take a backward glance as we cleared the Springfield city limits heading north. Back in Argyle, she moved into the spare bedroom and proceeded to irritate the crap out of everyone. Mom started staying late at the office to do the work she used to bring home. Our cat, Meow, stopped coming out of the basement except at meal times. Julie and my other friends stopped coming over. And I started studying up on undetectable household poisons. Only Lutefisk, our goldfish, liked her. But that ended when Selma fed him to death.

Eventually, Mom had to admit that Selma had to go. "After New Year's I'll find a group home for her," Mom said.

"New Year's?" I whined. "It's only October."

"I know. I know. But the holidays are going to be particularly hard on Selma this year. I don't want to press ahead too soon."

"Maybe I'll just move out," I grumbled.

"Shauna, just be patient. We're all doing the best we can. Especially Selma."

Especially, nothing. I was doing all the work. Which brings me back to the Friday night I dropped the plate and Selma decided it could be our secret forever and ever.

Cleaning up the debris and finishing the dishes took me exactly four minutes, leaving twenty until kickoff. I pulled the stopper from the sink and ran for my room. Selma could look after herself; I had to go.

I pulled on Lenny's spare jersey, grabbed my coat, and headed for the garage. Passing the living room, I called: "I've got to go, Selma. Mom will be home in a little while. Just find something—"

"I'm all ready."

I stopped and stared. Selma was in the hall, coat on, purse in hand, a bright orange stocking cap on her head. "What are you doing?" I bleated.

"Going to the game with you."

"But—"

"I like football. Mum-Mum and I used to go to every game at the high school. And we'd watch games on TV Saturday and Sunday and sometimes Monday night, but I couldn't stay up to the end of those Monday games because Mum-Mum had a rule about no TV after nine-thirty."

"But, Selma, it's real cold out tonight. Why don't you stay here where it's warm? I'll find a good movie for you. Or you can listen to the game on the radio." Oh, please, please, don't do this to me, Selma.

Selma frowned. "But I can't stay here. Mum-Mum never let me stay home alone. Even after I was all grown up."

"But—"

"She said I might let some strange man touch me and that she wouldn't have that in her house. So I always went with Mum-Mum everywhere."

Sixteen minutes to kickoff and I was hopelessly stuck

with Selma. Thanks, Mom. "Okay, okay. I'll leave a note for Mom. Wait in the car."

Dashing off the note and locking the door burned two more precious minutes. Selma was sitting in the front seat of the car, patiently waiting for me to help her with her seat belt. "Can't you do anything yourself, Selma? It's just a seat belt."

"Mum-Mum always said—"

"Forget it." I wrestled her seat belt into place, snapped it, started the car, shifted into reverse, and started backing down the driveway.

"You didn't lock the doors."

"So what? We're just going a little ways."

"Mum-Mum always—"

I slammed on the brakes, leaned across Selma to lock her door, locked my own, and started backing out.

"Watch for cars," Selma said. "You don't want to run into some strange man."

"Right," I said, dropped it in drive, and floored it.

The teams were huddling on the sidelines in preparation for the kickoff when I hustled Selma through the gate into the stadium. I pointed at the adult section. "There are seats up there. I'll see you after the game."

"But I want to sit with you and Julie."

"But you're not a student, Selma. And nobody *sits* in the student section. They stand up for the whole game."

"I don't mind."

"But, Selma! You're an adult. I'm a kid. You can't—" I

paused and stared into her pleading eyes. "I suppose there might be a strange man up there, huh?"

She nodded emphatically.

I sighed. "Okay. Come on."

We wedged our way through the crowd toward the space Julie had saved for me. "Hi, Julie!" Selma waved furiously.

Julie gaped. "Oh, hi, Selma." She looked at me.

"Don't ask," I said.

While Selma got her purse stowed under the seat, Julie leaned in close. "What's she doing here?"

"I told you not to ask."

"Like I'm going to pay attention to that. What's going on?"

"Mom isn't back from a showing in Wausau, and Selma can't stay home alone. Ignore her."

"I don't think that's going to be easy."

Too true. I could have brought a crocodile on a leash into the student section and created less of a stir. Around us kids shifted uncomfortably, whispered, took furtive glances at Selma. If there had been a rock nearby, I would have crawled under it.

Out on the field Sid Halverson got ready to kick off. Thank God, I thought. In a moment everybody will forget about Selma.

Uh-huh. That was what I thought before Selma produced the cowbell from her enormous purse. My eyes must have bugged half out of my head, but before I could summon my wits to say anything—as in *Oh, God, Selma, please, please, please don't!*—Sid kicked the ball and Selma started ringing the bell for all she was worth.

Julie grabbed me from the other side. "Lenny's going to get him!"

Lenny had slipped through the throng of blockers trying to protect the kid who'd fielded the kick. The kid ducked away, headed for the sidelines, but Lenny made a flying dive to bring him down by the ankles. As usual, I held my breath until he bounced up grinning. Beside me Selma jumped up and down, screeching in time with the bell.

I felt more than heard my cell phone. I stuck a finger in one ear and answered.

"Shauna? It's Mom. What's all—"

"I can't hear you," I shouted.

"What's all the noise?"

"The *game*, Mom. I'm at the *game*."

"Where's—"

"What?"

"Where's Selma?"

"She's here with me."

"At the game?"

"*Yes*, at the *game*. She's ringing a cowbell. Come and get her, Mom."

"I'm sorry, dear, but—"

"Mom, I'm going to die if you don't! I just know it!"

"I can't, dear. I'm still in Wausau."

"But when will you be home?"

"Tomorrow morning. I'm at the Shorewood Motel tonight."

"But Mom!"

"I'm going to hang up, dear. I can barely hear you."

I stared at the dead phone. That was it. There was absolutely nothing to do but throw myself from the top of the stadium . . . and take Selma with me. I glared at her.

Out on the field the Holman running back fumbled the ball, and six of our guys jumped on it. Julie screeched: "Ring the bell, Selma! Ring the bell!" Selma did. Okay, I'd kill them both, then throw myself from the top of the stadium.

We won the game by a touchdown. Lenny survived unhurt, making a few tackles and grinning up into the stands after every one. I knew he was smiling at me, and I guess that's why I committed neither murder nor suicide. But survival meant another Selma crisis. What was I to do with her while Lenny and I and about two dozen other jocks and their girls went out for pizza? Fear not; Julie had it all figured out. "You can sit with me and Randy, Selma," she said. "You'll like him."

Selma rode with Julie, which left me a few minutes to break the news to Lenny. He came bounding out of the locker room and jogged across the parking lot to me. "Hi," he said. "Was that a great game or what?"

"Yeah, it was," I said. "You played really well."

"All for you." He leaned over for a kiss.

I broke it off a lot shorter than I would have liked. "Lenny, I've got bad news. Selma's along tonight. She rode with Julie to Pizza Maestro."

"Selma? As in your mom's cousin Selma?"

"The one and the same."

"This is a joke, right?"

"God, I wish it were. Mom's gone overnight, and I had to bring Selma to the game."

"Why? Can't she stay at home alone?"

"Nope, she's afraid of strange men."

"Oh. . . ." He shrugged, turning philosophical—which left me feeling abandoned. "Well, nothing much we can do about it, I guess."

"We could run away. Live out our lives on some desert island."

"Maybe later. I'm too hungry right now. Let's go eat pizza."

I nodded hopelessly and started the car.

"You know," he said, "something funny happened tonight. There was somebody up in the stands ringing a bell, sort of a cowbell or something."

"Oh, I know," I said.

"Well, it really helped. We thought it was funny, but it irritated the crap out of the Holman guys. I think that's part of the reason they never seemed to get on track. I mean, we really thought we were going to get waxed tonight, but we beat 'em. I wonder who that person was."

"I think you're about to find out."

"Huh?"

"Never mind. Tell me about the game."

Selma was the bell-ringing hero, the toast of the party, the talk of the town. All the kids made a big deal of her.

Probably a dozen adults came over to the table to compliment her. When we finally got home around midnight, she was still pumped. "I never thought people would like my cowbell so much. People in Springfield never said anything."

"Good for them," I said.

Selma tilted her head to study me. "Didn't you like my bell, Shauna?"

"It's just that I used to enjoy being able to hear out of my right ear."

"Did your ear get cold?"

"Forget it," I said.

The Saturday newspaper called Selma the "Mystery Cowbell Lady" and featured a big picture of her on the front page of the sports section. I was there, too, standing beside her looking sour.

When Mom came in around noon, Selma waved the paper at her exultantly. "Look, Elly, I'm the Cowbell Lady!"

Mom read the headline out loud: "'Mystery Cowbell Lady Inspires Argyle Upset of Holman.' Why are you a mystery? Didn't the photographer ask your name?" (That's my mom, cuts right to the heart of things.)

Selma giggled. "Nobody asked me anything. I think everybody was too excited about the game. Isn't that a nice name? The Cowbell Lady?"

I stared heavenward. Mom laughed. "Well, it has a *ring* to it."

"*Mom,*" I said threateningly. "This is *not* the time."

"Oh," she said, "you're in a bad mood." She looked at the picture again. "You certainly don't look like you were having fun when this was taken. Was something the matter?"

I was going to have to add Mom to my hit list, right up there with Selma, Julie, and a certain newspaper photographer. "Mom," I said, "we need to talk." I headed for my bedroom.

"Just let me get a cup of coffee and read about the game. Then I'll be in."

I was lying on my bed staring a hole through the ceiling when she came in. "What's the matter, dear?"

"Do you really have to ask, Mom? I was stuck with Selma the whole evening. The biggest day of the week, and I'm babysitting a fifty-three-year-old child with a cowbell."

She smiled. "Well, it seems she had fun."

"But I didn't, Mom! As you might have noticed, I've got a boyfriend these days. And I'm trying to fit in with his crowd so I can keep him for a while. Because, as you also might have noticed, I've been just a little bit bored sitting around with you, Selma, and Emily Dickinson for company on Friday nights."

"You went out with your girlfriends quite a bit. You and Julie and—"

"Don't confuse this with facts, Mom! We are talking about serious girl-boy stuff and the fact that you stuck me with Selma last night."

"Oh, it wasn't really that bad, was it?"

"It was worse! She made a spectacle of herself and

embarrassed me in front of just about everybody in school."

"I thought she was supposed to be a hero—the 'Mystery Cowbell Lady.'" She laughed.

"You are not taking this seriously, Mom. I am really mad at you."

She managed to stifle her smile. "I'm sorry, dear. But, you know, we do have to eat. And that means I have to go out of town on business sometimes."

"But you said you'd be home by suppertime."

"Well, I didn't anticipate . . . a couple of complications."

A spot of color appeared just below her right cheekbone, triggering all my feminine intuition. "Wait a second! What complications?"

"Well, I ran into an old friend."

"As in male friend."

"Yes, as in male friend. Now don't get upset. We didn't stay at the motel together or anything. We just went out, had a nice supper, and talked."

I gazed at her, trying to summon all my indignation, then slumped back on the bed. "Okay, tell me about him."

"Well, he's a broker for a firm in Rhinelander. We were on a panel together at a conference a couple of years ago . . ."

And my mother told me about her romance while I went back to staring at the ceiling and wondering exactly why I was so miserable.

At least I had Lenny to myself on Saturday night. We rented two vampire DVDs and did a double feature at his house with a byte of time off now and then for our own necking. (I know. I'm sorry.)

Sunday morning I went with Mom and Selma to church. "Gee, maybe you ought to bring your cowbell," I said to Selma. She giggled.

"Shauna, some things aren't for joking about," Mom said.

Well, whoop-de-whooping-do, I thought.

As soon as we finished Sunday dinner, Mom rushed off to do a showing, leaving me with the dishes and the Mystery Cowbell Lady. Selma must have been feeling pretty adventurous, because she actually found the right channel for the Packer game all by her little self. Then she picked up Saturday's newspaper and stared for about the eight-thousandth time at her picture.

It was then that I snapped, "Hey, Mystery Cowbell Lady, why don't you get your butt over here and be the Mystery Dish-Wiping Lady for a while?"

She dropped the newspaper and sort of shrank back into her chair. "I couldn't."

I scowled at her. "What do you mean you couldn't?"

She licked her lips. Had she actually gone a little pale?

"Mum-Mum wouldn't—"

I tossed the towel in disgust on the counter. "Forget it! I'll wash and wipe them myself later." I stalked off to my bedroom to write a paper for English.

Even when I'm upset, I'm usually pretty good at concentrating. So it was a while before I registered an odd *tink-tink-tink* mixed in with the sound of the football game on the TV in the living room. I tiptoed down the hall, the noise getting louder the closer I got to the living room. I peeked in and saw Selma, her face ecstatic, wildly ringing her cowbell for the end of the first half.

Maybe it was the unbelievable happiness I saw on her face that made me leave the sarcasm out of my voice. "What's wrong with your bell?" I asked.

She jumped, set down the bell with a *clank* on the table beside her, and clasped her hands in her lap. "I'm sorry, Shauna! Really. I tried not to make noise. I won't do it anymore. Just don't take it." And she started to cry.

I sat down slowly in a chair near her and tried to think of something to say. I mean, I'd seen Selma bury her mom without crying like this. "Selma, don't cry. I'm not going to take your cowbell. You're . . . well, you're the Cowbell Lady. You've got to have your cowbell."

She nodded furiously, not looking at me.

"I just asked what you did to make it so quiet? I mean, I hardly heard it."

She picked up the cowbell, turned it to show me the wad of tissue stuck inside. "I didn't want to disturb you," she said. "I'm sorry, Shauna. I really am."

My brain was at last starting to make a few connections. "Did you really take your cowbell to the games in Springfield?"

Selma bit her lip, then shook her head. "I wanted to but Mum-Mum said I'd make too much noise and that strange men might—"

"Might stare at you."

She nodded. "Or maybe try to touch me."

I thought of asking more about all the strange men who seemed to obsess Great-Aunt Melba but decided the time wasn't quite right. "Selma, did Mum-Mum let you help with the dishes?"

"Oh, no! I broke a plate when I was a real little girl. Kind of like you did. And she made me sit all afternoon in the pantry with my hands like this." She held up her tightly clasped hands. "And after that I never got to help again."

"You know, Selma, Mum-Mum's dead."

"I know. She and Daddy are buried right next to each other. But they're really in Heaven with the baby Jesus."

"Selma, I don't know where they are. But I know you don't have to worry about Mum-Mum being mad at you anymore. You can help with the dishes here. You could, I don't know, learn to bake cookies or something. And . . . ," I had to take a breath because—God—this was tough, "and you can take your cowbell to the football games and ring it as loud as you want to."

Selma looked at me, her eyes again brimming with tears. I thought she was going to say something about the cowbell, but instead she said, "I'm afraid I'd drop a plate."

Okay, this next part is corny, but, heck, we needed some new dishes anyway. "Come on," I said. She followed me into the kitchen. I dug into the cupboard, pulling out the two most chipped, cracked, and ugly plates from our garage-sale hoard of china. I handed her one. "Okay," I said, "this is for Mum-Mum." I dropped my plate, which broke, rather disappointingly, into only a few dozen pieces.

Selma stared at me, eyes wide, her plate clutched in her hands. "Go ahead, Mystery Cowbell Lady," I said. "This can be our secret, too."

Selma started giggling then and stretched as high as she could, all the way up on her tiptoes and, still giggling, she let the plate drop. And, gosh, it made a lovely noise smashing into a million gazillion pieces.

Oh, yeah, the strange-man mystery. Selma told me all about it while we were doing the dishes together Monday evening. Mum-Mum had been warning her about strange men all her life. But then a neighbor who'd lost his wife started helping Selma and Mum-Mum with their yard work. And after a while, Selma stopped worrying about him being a strange man and they started getting pretty friendly.

"Was this a long time ago?" I asked.

"Oh, no. Maybe . . ." She thought. "Maybe about three years ago."

"Three years ago? Which meant you were, like, fifty?"

"Uh-huh. He was older. Sixty-two, he told me."

"And you two got involved?"

She tilted her head. "I don't know what—"

"You know, like sweethearts."

She giggled. "Oh, nothing like that. We liked to sit on the porch together. Sometimes we'd hold hands. Or maybe he'd put his arm around me. And a couple of times he kissed me. He had kind of a prickly upper lip."

"And Mum-Mum didn't like you doing anything like that."

"Uh-uh. She made him go away. She said he was a strange man and that she'd call the police if he came around again."

"Do you think he was a strange man, Selma?"

She hesitated. "He never did anything bad to me. But Mum-Mum said he would if we let him hang around."

And of course you believed her. "Whatever happened to him?"

"I guess he's still in Springfield. I've got a picture I could show you."

"Why don't you write to him?"

"Oh, I couldn't—" she started to say, then began furiously wiping a plate. After a long minute, she said quietly, mostly to herself I think: "Mum-Mum's dead."

That night we found his address on the Internet, and I helped Selma write him a letter.

Four days later, on a Friday evening just before supper, I answered the doorbell to find a short, bald guy with shy blue eyes standing on the stoop, baseball cap in his hands. "You're not—" I said, though Selma had showed me his picture.

He lifted his shoulders, let them drop, and grinned. "I'm afraid so."

I tried to keep the hysterical laughter out of my voice. "Mom, Selma, come here. You are *not* going to believe this."

So where do you suppose the reunited lovers chose to go on a Friday night in Argyle, Wisconsin? You got it, the high school football game, where they sat holding hands in the adult section and Selma, the really-not-so-mysterious Cowbell Lady, rang her cowbell like she wanted all the world to hear.

THE DOUGHNUT BOOTS HIS REPUTATION

Featuring:
Randy "the Doughnut" Schmidtke,
  offensive tackle and diaper changer
Julie Cecil, *girlfriend and job counselor*
Lexi, *little person*
Sluggo, *a dog*

For about the twentieth time that day, I stared miserably at the form for volunteer hours. Julie nudged me with an elbow.

"Go ahead, Randy. What's the harm?"

"The guys would laugh at me."

"So what? If it's what you want to do, do it."

"I've got to think some more about it."

"You've been thinking about it for a week, and it's due at the end of the day. Go ahead and fill it out. Besides, who's going to give Randy Schmidtke, the one and only Doughnut, a lot of crap about what he chooses to do for volunteer hours?"

She was right, of course. That's what happens when you have a girlfriend about ten times smarter than you are. But I still couldn't make myself fill it out. "I'll do it later," I said.

"Chicken," she said.

I guess this whole mess started the night I took my old teddy bear away from my schnauzer. Sluggo didn't like giving it up and ran around me yapping. "I'm just borrowing it, Sluggo," I said. "I'll give it back. I promise."

He paused, tilted his head to one side, and gave me his furry-eyeball look.

"Give him a biscuit and he'll forget all about it," Mom said. "Hurry. We're running late."

I gave Sluggo a dog cookie, pulled on my coat, and followed her out to where my stepdad, Jake, had the car warming up. I held the door for her while she got her bulk into the front passenger's seat. She grunted with the effort.

"You okay?" Jake asked.

"Yes. But, boy, am I sick of being pregnant. Carrying Randy wasn't nearly this tough."

"That was quite a while ago. You probably just forgot."

"Some things a woman doesn't forget, Bozo."

I got myself wedged into the narrow backseat. Jake grinned at me. "She should complain, huh?"

"Yeah," I said. "Try being my size for a while."

"Don't you two start on me," Mom said. "Now come on. I don't want to be late."

"We've got plenty of time," Jake said, and dropped the car into gear.

I decided to give it one more try. "Are you really sure I should go, Mom? I mean, isn't this class really for little kids?"

"Oh, so you know all about helping to take care of a baby, huh?"

"Well, no. But I'm going to be the biggest one there."

Jake laughed. "Since when weren't you the biggest one everywhere?"

"But I wouldn't want to make the nurses uncomfortable," I said.

"I'm sure the nurses have had teenagers in class before," Mom said. "And you agreed you'd help take care of this baby."

Okay, I had. But a class on diapering? Give me a break, Mom. But she wasn't likely to. Nope, babies were serious business.

I guess I always knew that Mom would like a couple of kids besides me. She had me when she was seventeen and raised me by herself until Jake came along a couple of years ago. By that time I was fifteen and bigger than any other kid in the school. I'll hand it to them that they actually asked me if I'd mind if they had a kid together. And I didn't. Why should I? I've always liked kids. And it wasn't like I thought a baby in the house would be much of a problem.

Mom got different ideas when she learned about this family baby-care program at the hospital. She came home from the orientation meeting with some big news for me and Jake. Having a baby was a family project, responsibility, mission, and experience not to be missed by any member of the family, no matter how small. Or in my case, big. Which meant we were supposed to learn all sorts of stuff about baby care before the baby even got born. Jake looked at me. I looked at him. He shrugged. I shrugged. "Sure, honey," he said. "We're up for that."

"Randy?"

"Sure, Mom. No problem."

"Ha," she'd said. "I'll remember you said that."

Next stop, the sibling class. I objected, of course. But she wouldn't hear any of it. "You might as well work a little now than a lot more later. Find something you can practice diapering."

"Diapering?"

"Right. As in, cleaning the baby's bottom and putting on a new diaper. Ever hear of that?"

"I guess I could take Sluggo."

"If you don't mind losing a finger or two," Jake said.

Just then Sluggo came into the kitchen, dragging Mr. Teds by a foot. My old teddy bear was a little the worse for dog teeth, drool, and shaking by the neck. But at least he wouldn't bite.

By the time we parked in the hospital lot, I hadn't come up with a good reason—other than my size and age—for skipping the sibling class. Not that I didn't give it a shot when Mom and Jake split off to go to their Lamaze class. "Mom—" I started.

"Nope. You promised to go with the program. Your class is straight ahead. Room three."

I went.

All the kids in the room looked up from coloring pictures when I walked in. Not a one was more than five or six years old from what I could tell. I looked around, spotted an adult-sized chair, and sat, trying to look small. The kids whispered among themselves. A couple of them went back to coloring, but the other six or so thought I was more interesting. A skinny girl with bobbed hair marched up to me.

"Who are you?" she demanded.

"Randy."

"I'm Lexi. Are you here to help my mom?"

"Uh, no. Who's your mom?"

"She's the teacher. I'm her assistant. So, what are you doing here?"

"Taking the class."

Her eyes widened. "You're going to have a baby?"

"Well, not exactly. My mom's having a baby."

"*My* mom says everybody in the family has the baby. That's why everybody has to work together."

"Uh, yeah. Right. I agree."

"Good. Did you bring a doll or a stuffed animal to diaper?"

I produced Mr. Teds from under my coat.

"Yuck," she said. "What'd you do to it? Throw up on it or something?"

"My dog kind of chewed on it. It's been his for a while."

"And you took it back?"

"Well, I borrowed it. I gave him a biscuit."

She pursed her lips. "Well, I guess that's okay, then."

A nurse hurried in, her arms filled with bottles, diapers, and what all. She paused when she saw me. "May I help you?"

"I'm here for the class."

Her eyebrows shot up an inch or so. "Oh. Well, that'll be a little different. Okay, children, first we're going to learn how to diaper a baby. Lexi will pass out diapers and baby wipes. I'll hand out towels and baby powder. Put your doll or stuffed animal on the towel and then look up here."

All the kids who weren't already sitting on the floor got down on it. I joined them, feeling like Shrek. Just not as green. With Mr. Teds lying on the towel, I looked up to watch the demonstration.

Now I'm an offensive lineman. Which means my fingers are always a little bashed up. And I'm not exactly the handiest person anyway. But after watching Lexi's mom diaper a doll a couple of times, I figured I could handle getting a diaper on Mr. Teds. It proved trickier than I thought.

Lexi plopped down across from me. "No, no. You've got it on backward." She took Mr. Teds, turned the diaper around, and paused. "Did you wipe his bottom?"

"Uh, no. I kind of forgot that part."

"You can't forget or he'll get a rash. Let's start from the beginning."

After a couple of tries, I started getting the hang of things. And it was fun. I even messed up a couple of times on purpose, just so Lexi could correct me in her patient I'm-the-teacher voice.

We moved on to the wrapping-the-baby-in-a-blanket unit. Then we did the giving-the-baby-a-bottle-without-burning-the-crap-out-of-him/her unit. Then, with three different colored stars on our foreheads, we each got a certificate showing we were certified siblings. I was last in line. Lexi's mom grinned at me. "You're a good sport. Lexi will talk all week about you."

"It's been fun."

"Kids *are* fun. This is really your first little brother or sister?"

"Uh-huh. It's going to be a boy. Mom had one of those amnio things."

"Amniocentesis. And all is well?"

"Yeah, fine."

"Well, your little brother is going to have a great big brother. And I don't mean just your size. You've got a way with kids."

I looked around at the kids. "I, uh, never paid much attention to them before. They were just kind of these little people running around."

"And that's what they are. Little people. A lot of adults forget that. Well, thanks for coming. That was pretty courageous of you."

"Thanks for having me. I really enjoyed it."

"Don't forget that you have those stars on your forehead. You might want to take them off before you go out in public."

"Na, I think I'll leave them on for tonight."

Six weeks later Jake Junior was born. He's almost eighteen months old now. Sluggo doesn't know how to diaper JJ or give him a bottle, but between us we do a pretty good job taking care of him. Mom and Jake haven't been too bad at it either. The five of us are a family. Not that we weren't a family when it was just Mom, Jake, Sluggo, and me. But it's better now, especially with Mom and Jake trying to get another baby going.

Me? I'm a senior. Next year I'm going to the community college so I can live at home for another couple of years. Of course, I have to graduate from high school first. But with Julie keeping on me about studying, my grades are pretty good. So all that's standing in the way is these stupid twenty-five volunteer hours I need to earn. At first I figured I'd just volunteer to take tickets at basketball games or something. Then last week I ran into Lexi's mom while I was getting gas at Quick Trip. "Hi. Remember me?" I asked.

"How could I forget you? You were the biggest student I ever had, and a star pupil, too."

"All us kids got stars."

"True. But you definitely stood out. So how do you like being a big brother?"

"It's great. We have a blast."

"I knew you would."

I hesitated. "Say, you wouldn't be doing any classes this winter, would you?"

"Two a week. I always get kids. It's a way for couples in Lamaze to save on a babysitter."

"Do you suppose I could help out? You see, I need these volunteer hours . . ." I explained.

"Sure. Love to have you."

So there it was. All I had to do was fill out the form and turn it in. But then I started worrying about my reputation.

Julie leaned over to whisper in my ear. "Randy, you know and I know and everybody else knows that you're not really a doughnut. You're a cream puff. Now go with it. Fill out the form. You won't be sorry."

I sighed, nodded, and got the form out of my pocket. Well, what the heck. I couldn't be just a dumb, macho jock forever.

"You know," Julie said, "maybe you ought to major in elementary ed in college. You could become the world's biggest kindergarten teacher."

"Uh-huh."

"No, I mean it. Just think—"

"I already have," I said. And signed.

A GOOD GAME

Featuring:
Ken Bauer, *tight end*
Rollin Acres, *fullback*
Steve Haupt, *linebacker*
Marvin "the Catman" Katt, *jerk*

A t the locker-room door, Sarah hopped up on tiptoe to give me a quick kiss. "Have a good game. Remember to wear your helmet. You, too, Rollin." She hurried off to find the pep band.

Rollin grinned. "Love that girl. Always got our best interests in mind. . . . Whoops, heeere's Steve!"

Steve Haupt came galloping down the hall in his uniform from Argyle East, the crosstown team. "Hey, guys!" he shouted. "Coach says we're gonna whup ya." He grinned his big, moon-faced grin.

We laughed. "You can try, Steve," I said. We gave him fives.

"You're tight end," he said to me.

"Three years," I said. "This is it. Last game."

"And you're the fullback," he said to Rollin.

"You got it, Steve," Rollin said.

Steve grinned, proud of his knowledge. "I'm a linebacker."

"You bet," I said.

"I gotta go. Have a good game, guys."

"You, too, Steve," we said.

"Yeah, me, too." He rushed on toward the field where he would, as always, be the first player to arrive—though he'd never played a single down.

"Quite the piece of work," Rollin said.

"Yeah," I said. "Happy guy."

"Listen up!" Coach Carlson yelled. The din in the locker room settled. "Now before we go over the game plan, I'm going to confirm a rumor: Steve Haupt is going to play tonight. He's been sitting on the East bench for three years, and this is his last game. Coach Kreuger wants to put him in for a series at left outside linebacker. I've promised not to call any plays that might involve Steve, so obviously we're only going to run plays to our left side. That way Steve doesn't get hurt, and he can't lose the game for his team, either."

Catman raised his hand. "What do we get out of this, Coach?"

"The satisfaction of doing the right thing."

"Yeah, but it's not our fault he's retar—"

I cut him off. "It's called Down syndrome, Catman. And it's not his fault, either. I say we give him his series."

About a dozen guys echoed me. Anyone who played sports at either high school in town knew Steve. He was at every game and meet, cheering West teams just as loudly as East teams, even when they played each other.

Rollin said, "Yeah. Come on, Catman. Surprise us and do something decent for a change."

Catman shut up, but he didn't look happy.

On the way onto the field, I waved to Sarah in the pep band section, and she gave me a *ta-ta-ta-dat-ta-daa* on her trumpet. Game time. Let Steve have his series. Otherwise, time to kick some butt.

At two wins and six losses, East wasn't much of a team. But this game was about bragging rights, and it was tough from the opening kickoff. Catman picked me out for three passes in the first half. And though he was a jerk—a fact appreciated by everybody who knew him—he could drill a pass hard enough to leave a dent.

It was 14–14 at the half when we went in to examine our bumps, bruises, scrapes, and sprains. Catman stalked about the locker room. "Come on, guys! We're letting these turkeys play with us. We've gotta bear down. We've gotta—"

"Catman," I said, "sit down and shut up. We know what we've got to do." There was a chorus of agreement from the other guys. Catman sat down, still not looking happy.

Late in the third quarter, Rollin broke two tackles and turned a three-yard plunge into a twenty-yard score to put us up 20–14. But East blocked the extra point.

We held and got the ball back a couple of minutes into the fourth quarter. When East took a time-out, Coach Carlson called us together. "Okay, I just got word that Steve Haupt is going in for the next three plays. Remember, run everything left, away from Steve."

"I think we ought to run right at him," Catman said.

Coach almost lost it. "Katt, we are *not* getting that boy hurt. Now forty-four belly left. Do it!"

I took my position at the right end of the line and looked over to see Steve. He was so excited that I thought his helmet was going to pop off any second. "Hey, Kenny," he hissed. "I'm in the game."

I grinned at him. "You sure enough are. Stay onside now."

Catman called: "Ready! Set. Hut, hut, *hut* . . ."

On the third *hut* he got the ball and handed off to Rollin, who rumbled off to the left side, where Steve wasn't, and gained us five yards.

Steve didn't do anything on the play, but there isn't much for an outside linebacker to do on a forty-four belly away from him. "Rollin got it," Steve called to me when the linemen untangled.

"Yep," I said. "Pretty good gain, too."

"Maybe you'll get it next."

"Maybe," I said. "You watch for the pass." I jogged back to our huddle.

Coach sent in the next play: forty-four keeper left. "All right," Catman said, "on two."

We ran the play, Catman faking the handoff to Rollin and keeping it himself. He tried to get outside the end, but East's right linebacker got there and stuffed him big time for a two-yard loss. Steve never made it into the play, while I made sure their left defensive end stayed out of it.

Catman was a regular furball of fury when he staggered into the huddle. The next play came in from Coach: thirty-one sweep left, a tailback play. "Nuts," Catman said. "That sweep hasn't worked all night. I'm calling the next play. It's eighty-one boot pass right."

I stared at him. An eighty-one boot right was a pass to the tight end. Me. "Hey," I said, "that'll put me up against Steve."

"Right! Run over him and get us a first down."

"No way! You throw it, I won't catch it."

"Hurry up, you two," Rollin said. "We're gonna get a delay of game."

Catman glared at me. "All right. We'll do it Coach Wimp's way. Thirty-one sweep left on two."

We broke the huddle and hustled to the line. Steve was still at left linebacker, still grinning, still prouder than anyone in the world. Up at the line, Catman had a weird look on his face. I should have known he was going to pull something.

He yelled: "Ready! Set! Red eighty-one! Red eighty-one! Hut, hut . . ." Catman had called an audible, changing the play back to the tight-end pass I'd told him I wouldn't catch. I sprinted into the flat and cut right hard, hearing Steve panting to keep up. The ball came out just a little high but catchable. I let it go off my fingers.

I should have batted it into the ground. Footballs have a funny shape, and they don't behave like other balls. Instead of skipping off my hands and sailing safely out of bounds, this particular football decided to do a back flip over my left shoulder. I swatted at it, lost my balance, and hit the ground as the crowd roared. I rolled and hopped up. What the hey were they cheering about? Then I saw Steve being pulled to his feet by a couple of teammates, his arms still wrapped around the ball he'd plucked from midair.

Hang around football for a few years and you'll see a lot of angry people. But I'd never seen anyone quite as mad as Coach Carlson. He came storming over to Catman. "What were you thinking, Katt? Look at me, young man!"

"It was third and seven, Coach. We needed yards."

"I sent you a sweep that was going to get them! And we had fourth down if we needed it. Now we've given them the ball, and they're revved up!"

Catman glared at me. "Bauer should have—"

"Don't even start," Coach snapped. "Sit down! You're not playing any more tonight!"

Coach yelled for Jim Braehm. Jim grabbed a ball and started warming up with Rollin. After a minute, I wandered over to catch a couple.

East drove the ball down our throats for the next five minutes, taking every second they could off the clock. When they finally scored to take the lead 21-20, we only had three minutes to get it back. Jim Braehm played his heart out. We all did. But we ran out of time, gas, and downs thirty yards short of their goal line.

In the locker room, Catman got after me. "You could have caught that pass!"

"It was high."

"It wasn't that high. You made a better catch in the first quarter. You missed that ball on purpose!"

"Well, you'll never really know, will you?"

"And so little Stevie gets an interception. Did you plan that part?"

"Nope. But weird things can happen out there in the flat."

"And it doesn't bother you to lose your last game as a senior, huh? You can just blow it off?"

I spun on him. "Yeah, it bothers me! But I didn't throw the ball that lost it for us. *You* did. But, hey, Catman.

Maybe you shouldn't mind so much. You made Steve a hero tonight. You ought to be proud of that, because it's gonna be one of the high points of his life. You? You're gonna play another year. You're gonna have a lot of high points. But, you know something? You're never going to be a hero. Not to anybody who knows you. You can't hide it, Catman. You're a jerk!"

We glared at each other. From the bench behind me, Rollin sighed and said, "Beat it, Catman. Ken, get dressed. We're out of here."

Catman, who didn't seem to have a lot more to say anyway, took his advice. So did I.

We left the locker room tired and angry. In the jammed hallway outside, we ran into Steve. He broke away from the crowd and came rushing up to us. "I caught it!" He threw his arms around Rollin and then hugged me.

"Yeah, Steve, you caught it," I said.

"You guys played great! We had fun."

I hesitated.

Rollin smiled. "Yeah, we sure did, Steve. A lot of fun."

"See you," he shouted. We watched as he was swept away by the crowd of people wanting to shake his hand.

Rollin said, "You know, I didn't buy it when you were laying it on Catman, but maybe it really was worth losing just to see Steve win."

"I didn't believe it either," I said. "But maybe it was."

Rollin slapped me on the shoulder. "Anyway, Steve's got it right. We had fun. I'll see you at the dance."

"Sure," I said. "Good game, Rollin."

He turned, grinning. "Hey, they *all* were. Win or lose, they *all* were."

"Yeah," I said. "They were."

We laughed and shook hands. And feeling a whole lot better, I pushed out the doors to the parking lot. Sarah was sitting on the hood of the Green Hammer, waiting for me. I grinned and waved. I didn't need any consoling. Not tonight. Not with a harvest moon rising like a great orange lamp over autumn and the end of the season.